HAVE A NYC 2
New York Short Stories

Edited by Peter Carlaftes & Kat Georges

THREE ROOMS PRESS
New York, NY

Have a NYC 2

First Edition

ISBN: 978-0-9884008-4-9

Editors: Peter Carlaftes & Kat Georges

Cover and Interior Design:
KG Design International
katgeorges.com

Published by
Three Rooms Press, New York, NY
threeroomspress.com

To the memory of
Edward Irving Koch

INTRODUCTION

Taking on the streets. East or Westside. Uptown and Down. The pace quickens through the boroughs from necessity. Every move the most important. Too much competition. Looking at each other for someone to blame. Doing anything just to be part of the magnitude. Everybody lost in the expanse. The City doesn't cheat you. It teaches. You absorb either knowledge or blows.

There are days when you find out you can't cut it anymore. And there are others when you come out at the top. Living life as only life was really meant to be lived. And the magic lasts forever till it stops. Perhaps you'll make it in the City. Time will tell. That's your story.

CONTENTS

FINDERS AND KEEPERS
BY PETER CARLAFTES

They were coming for him. Really. Searching every floor room by room. Matter of time before they found him. Yet inside he believed they never would. So trying best to hold his breath, he kept perfectly still.

This is how the light hit him most every morning. Dripping sweat and fear. But somehow he always got up and ate breakfast with the others and then dutifully strode outside and started cleaning off the sidewalk in front of the building with the pressure hose. Staring into the skyline across the East River trying to remember how his life had been spent. All he knew is they called him Taylor.

Projects Counselor Kevin Yula was looking out the window of his office and thinking along similar lines—he didn't know what to make of this withdrawn curiosity who just showed up outside the Borden Avenue Veteran's Residence and started helping Old Man Otis clean the walk nearly 10 weeks ago.

When Old Man Otis first asked him, What's your name?, the stranger answered, I don't know. The only identification the man possessed was a worn-down bent dog tag they could only make out the name Taylor from. They didn't know if the tag was even his. Is Taylor your name?

I don't know. Old Man Otis thought the man was probably wanted by the law.

Taylor was tall—6'3", with lanky body going gaunt and a thin, hawkish face topped by coarse black hair which strangely seemed recently cut. Maybe 30–35. You couldn't tell, and if you asked him, Taylor answered, I don't know. Same as when you asked him, Where you from?

Yula took an immediately liking to Taylor. Especially since Old Man Otis had a setback with dialysis and was sent off that same week to Brooklyn Veteran's Hospital indefinitely. So after Taylor proved that he could handle the old man's duties responsibly two days running, Yula had an orderly set up a cot in an unused examination room for Taylor to have a place to live and sleep. So far, so good. He rapped his right set of knuckles on his desk, which wasn't wood.

There was nothing at all strange about some homeless vet ending up at a shelter like the Borden Avenue Residence, thought Yula—but how did Taylor ever find this impossible-to-reach-by-foot one hemmed in by Newtown Creek and the L.I.E.? Maybe down the line they'd learn the answer. But for now, Yula had to get back to (as he liked to quote Yogi) his *half the job is 80 percent* paperwork.

Taylor unclenched the hose handle and gazed at the buildings across the river. He knew that they were more alive than him. More heroic. There was silence with him now. Sometimes—the explosion. Such a loud and deafening sound.

Boom! And just like that the two were gone. What two? Gone where? The quiet didn't tell.

He started rolling up the hose.

His next job was to sweep around the dumpsters at the back end of the parking lot along the west side of the building, which he finished with diligence. Then he saw a good-sized rat emerge between a warped stack of rotting palettes and start nosing through the muddy field behind the 10-foot chain-link fence topped with razor wire. Then a dark grey feral cat suddenly pounced and the rat quickly scurried back between palettes while the cat took position, enjoying the smell of fear in its prey. Which all of a sudden Taylor smelled, too. So he focused on the cat perched to strike in an instant and became what the cat was right then.

Awareness. Immediacy. What a smell fear holds. Power. Hear the scraping? Patience. This is my domain. Wait. Feel the creature cower. It will soon make a dash for survival. It will lose. And my hunger will be sated. If its meat is good enough. I hear it moving closer to the edge. There it goes. The sound is deafening.

Taylor opened his eyes. Off to the left, two skinny boys in the field haunched laughing, one shouted, Neutered that Mo'Fucker, stuffing the pistol down in his waistband. Let me shoot the next one, begged the other. You suck my dick I let you, cracked the shooter, so the other shot back, Don't your Daddy do it for you?, as they scampered off east towards the creek out of view, paying him no mind at all.

Taylor turned his gaze to the cat's remains. If left there as is, the lucky rat would eat its carcass. Nothing certain till it ends. He started thinking about what might have caused those boys to act like that, so cold-blooded and without provocation. He started wishing for a world where living things were safe and one which made boys who'd never act in such a manner and to be as one such boy. Youth in bloom. His time began.

He knew exactly where he was. Standing at the middle front window staring out at Davidson Avenue. And to the right crossing Evelyn Place. A little boy of six years. Watching occasional people pass by. When a deep voice behind booms, Time to take a shower, Shawn. And the boy turns to look at the tall man approaching, who guides him off the window and pulls the curtains shut. He can see a torn green couch when he's led out of room into a hallway, passing the kitchen halfway down to the left where a small, round woman sitting at the table leans in to light a cigarette on the stove as they pass, and when the hall ends, they enter the bathroom with a big claw foot tub. Then the man turns on the water. The sound is deafening.

Taylor opened his eyes. Was that him—the boy called Shawn? Shawn Taylor? No bells. Well at least there were two streets he knew the names of now. Davidson Avenue and Evelyn Place. Maybe someone could help him locate where they were. But even if they could and that was him as a boy, it was so long ago there would be nothing left. Even a world of his own making let him down. He was starting to sweat. And he still had to bury the cat.

Kevin Yula saw Taylor walk past his office and felt at ease. He was sure that one day soon, the man would come around. Most do. He'd seen it happen before. But they're also broken people. They've seen combat. Horror. Dying. Taylor was one of them, too. Yula was glad he'd helped Taylor at least get situated with the basics and there was plenty of time to work him into the system when indeed he came around. He was glad that things were working out for now. And looking at the clock, Yula also knew that four hours from now he'd be getting on the L.I.E. and since it was Saturday, he only had a short drive to Jamaica. With its own brand of horror. But definitely getting better all the time.

Taylor found a strong plastic bag and took the shovel out back through the field and stood over the cat's body, trying to remember what happened to the boy in the shower. Asking, How could a father ever do that to his son? And if this is the only world, then may he be someone who'd never do anything harmful to his or any boy.

The man stands under the streetlight on the west side of Haven Avenue staring up at the windows of apartment 3C. He takes the crumpled letter and reads it again in his mind—What happened to us, Tanya? Why can't we make things work out like we used to? I can't take this anymore. Why won't you speak to me? I know we got problems. Everybody's got problems. But what happens to Terrence? Why should he be kept from me? The man drops the letter, his eyes welling up with tears. Then his hand finds the butt of the gun. He looks back at the windows. There was no way he could hurt them. He walks up to the end of West 181st to see the river and the bridge. The water beckons. He takes the gun. The sound is deafening.

Taylor opened his eyes. He couldn't fit the pieces. If this was him of past, then how come he didn't die? Or was he dead? He didn't know. He rubbed the dog tag in his front left pocket and peered at the buildings across the East River. They were more alive than him and there was nothing he could do about that. Taylor opened the bag and set it on the ground right next to the cat. Then he shoveled its body right in and found some rocks nearby and added them to the bag to weigh it down and tied the end into a knot and walked down to the edge of Newton Creek and hurled the bag out as far as he could.

The sounds are deafening. The city is Fallujah. There are too many locals in the square to secure the area. Santos and Crenshaw walk warily in front of Taylor. The lieutenant motions them to spread out. A screaming man jumps out ahead. The sound is deafening.

The bag just kept sailing in super-slow motion as Taylor reached out to help his buddies, but they were gone as gone could get. They both died bleeding in that square. The bag finally hit the surface and sank. He opened his eyes. He knew the two names of the soldiers who died now. Taylor was coming around.

OVER HER DEAD BODY
BY THOMAS PRYOR

On a cold night in 1979, John's friends told him his girlfriend was leaving him for the star player on his rugby team. Lucinda looked like Gina Lollobrigida with a delicious dirty mouth and a wicked sense of humor. John woke with the same goal every morning, have sex with Lucinda twice and never take his eyes off that gorgeous face during the act. Her girlfriends had crushes on her. John's mother had a crush on her.

As the news pummeled him, one thought bulleted up. He had to move out of his parents Long Island home. The loneliness and depression he felt living in the suburbs would be unbearable without Lucinda. John missed the city's neighborhoods, and he was close to killing his insomniac woodworking father whose basement shop was directly under his bedroom. His dad made dollhouses and miniature furniture to fill the homes he built perfectly to scale. He sold his stuff to FAO Schwartz and other specialty stores along Lexington Avenue near Hunter College.

That night, around midnight John heard the saw and lathe start up beneath him and stomped his foot on the floor. "It's my house!" his father yelled up. His nerves shot, John mumbled, "Why don't you saw the friggin' house in half while you're at it." John got up, dressed and walked to the LIRR and took a train into Manhattan. He knew his father was right, it was his home, and he had to get out of there. Sleep deprivation and loneliness are miserable partners.

A few days later, Lucinda called John. "My Abuela died." With mixed feelings, John comforted her knowing they were finished. He told her he'd meet her at her grandmother's wake the next night in Brooklyn.

After work, John rode the R subway line to the last stop in Bay Ridge. Walking down East 92nd Street, he made a turn onto Third Avenue. Looking up, he saw a bright string of pearls strung across the dark December sky. His first peek at the Verranzano Bridge—it was close, clear, beautiful. To his left and right, were two and three story brick buildings lined with Mom and Pop stores. John smelled the salty bay.

His mind spun as he entered McLaughlin's Funeral Home with a St. Anthony mass card trapped in his armpit. Inside the viewing parlor, Lucinda took his coat and kissed him on the cheek. The men greeted John warmly and the women kissed him on the lips—their breath an explosive combination of garlic and perfume. Lucinda's family loved John. They considered him a calming influence in her life, her parents called her *poco loco en el coco*. Lucinda busted through the LIRR crossing gates with a carload of friends on a dare. On a steamy day at Rye Playland, she took off her skirt and blouse and gallivanted down the Midway in her underwear. At their rugby summer house she invited herself and John into a shower with their mutual friend, Linda, so they could finally settle the question whose breasts weighed more, John handled all four like prized coconuts. He sold his soul to be with Lucinda and figured he might be getting off easy by breaking up.

Lucinda's mom cornered him at a party, "John, I have $20,000 put away for Lucinda's wedding. If you elope, it's yours." One afternoon they were messing around on the floor while her parents went to a diner. They came back too fast; John and Lucinda dressed too quickly. The four of them stood awkwardly in the Levittown kitchen. Her parents stared at them strangely as John frantically tried to button Lucinda's 28-inch dungarees and she swam in his 32s. And they didn't kill John.

After saying hello to everyone at the wake, John approached the coffin, dropped to the kneeler and said a silly made up prayer (he didn't know the woman). "Dear Lord, please take care of this lady, Okee-Dokee?" Looking at the body he noticed an oversized jeweled rosary in her hands. The large Jesus on the cross seemed to be smirking at him.

John stood, turned and saw Lucinda's Uncle Jose. He was crying a little and he was the superintendent of grandma's house. John approached him.

"So sorry about Mom, Jose." John hugged him and said, "May I ask, is the apartment available?"

Jose looked at his mother, then back to John.

"I'm not sure. You want it? That'd be nice. Oh, there's Mr. Lanza, he owns the building."

John turned and saw a medium height man dressed in black with a fedora in his hand. Mr. Lanza went directly to the coffin and knelt to pay his respects. When he got up, John tugged his tie and closed the space.

"Hello, Mr. Lanza, I'm part of the family, is the apartment still available?"

"What apartment?"

John nodded towards the coffin.

"Ooooo, you want it?"

"Yes, I heard the rent is $148?"

"Nope, $185."

John swiftly shook his hand hard up and down like that picture of the Atlantic meeting the Pacific to complete the Continental Railroad. John wrote Mr. Lanza's phone number down on a *Five Stages of Loss* brochure sitting next to the plastic wake cards on the table with the lace doily.

The next weekend, Lucinda helped John paint the apartment, gave him a goodbye blowjob and they officially broke up. John was sad, lonely, and broke but he wasn't living on Long Island. He merged his low budget with certain comfort foods: Thomas' English Muffins, bacon bits, Russian dressing, individually-wrapped American cheese, and Campbell's Golden Mushroom Soup. John ate the same things every day—except for one beautiful break.

His next door neighbor, Mrs. Larsen, a sweet, old Norwegian woman, made an immense pound cake with powdered sugar once a week. She'd cool it on her airshaft windowsill facing his. He could literally reach over and steal it, but never did. The aroma filled his kitchen and when the cake settled, Mrs. Larsen cut a sturdy piece that overflowed a china plate and passed it to John over the air-shaft. They did most of their socializing that way and she was the best neighbor on earth if you made noise. He did.

John was single now, and Friday and Saturday nights his friends came over, partied hard and played loud tunes before going out to the Bay Ridge bars. Their festivities concluded with a go out song—extremely important to keep the mood going—and their song was always by The J Geils Band.

Boom, boom, boom
Somebody help me!
Boom, boom, boom
Somebody help me now!

At the top of their lungs they'd march out the door, down four flights of stairs, through the lobby singing the song out into the street.

Somebody help me find my baby, I said I've got to
find my baby right now...
I'm looking in the morning, I'm looking at night,
gotta find my baby, but she's no where in sight...

Things we're good with Mrs. Larsen, but not so good beneath John. Jose's daughter, Maria, lived there and loved to house clean to jumpy music & salsa early on Saturday and Sunday mornings: Tito Puente *Mambo Diablo* & Ray Barretto's *Watusi*, a song John enjoyed but not with death so near. The sound rose, and the pulse of the percussion and screeching horns located the heart of John's massive hangover and tore the skin off the walls of his brain. John's music stopped at 10 p.m. Maria's started before seven. This was unacceptable. After a half-hearted try at diplomacy, they began an Acme Product War.

On Friday and Saturday nights, Maria banged brooms and mops up against her ceiling, opened her windows and blasted salsa music up the airshaft.

John in the morning—

- 100-watt speakers face down on the floor at max volume.
- Construction boot marching over her bedroom with heavy strides.

11

• Dropped 20-lb dumb bells from waist height directly over her light fixtures.

When they saw each other they didn't say a word. If Maria was with her father, John faked a smile. Word had not gotten back to them about the breakup with Lucinda, and John desperately needed as much help from the super as possible—his apartment was begging for plumbing and electrical work and he was a mechanical idiot. He needed assistance before the cat was out of the bag.

One Saturday morning two months into their battle, John woke to low music that he didn't recognize . . . The sound got louder.

"Boom, boom, boom . . ."

What the . . . ? Cautiously, John listened.

"Boom, boom, boom . . ."

No? No!

"Somebody help me, Boom, boom, boom . . ."

Oh shit, oh no, oh shit, it was J Geils, his song, "Looking For a Love." His album, *The Morning After*. Maria had bought the record; now she was giving John the business!

Defeated, John heaved and started to keen, but slowly it turned into laughter. He got out of bed, put on his pants, and grabbed something on the way out. Down the flight of stairs he knocked on the door.

Maria answered with a stern face in an oversized blue robe. John held an item up and her frown turned to a half-smile when she saw he offered a fresh six-pack of Thomas' English Muffins. She took the muffins, asked him in for coffee and they negotiated peace. John would be quiet one night; Maria would be quiet one morning. They worked it out, and for the first time John felt like he was home.

CHERRY WOLLSTONECRAFT AND JUSTINE LUSCIOUS SAVE THE WORLD

BY RAE BRYANT

I ran to New York with a bug up my ass, an unhealthy sexual appetite and a way with isms. In short time, I could fuck and stand in front of a painting and hold a novel and say if I liked the fucking or the painting or the novel and spout the proper isms to support my critical stance. I never really needed to use the isms well or quote the isms correctly. All I needed to know were the titles of things.

A small press in Manhattan gave me an internship that didn't pay much but I still had a few thousand dollars from student loans so I worked part time at a bar at night and by day hunkered down in my editorial cubicle, hung over and sour. If anyone came close, I spouted isms until they went away. I recited them monotone and rhythmic like Asperger's. Deconstructionism, postmodernism, feminism, historicism, new criticism, objectivism, formalism, structuralism . . . People thought I was strange but some thought I was entertaining too, a wonder, so I had to ramp up my act. I started telling people I knew the square root of Freudianism's Oedipal paradigm and why Lacanian criticism would start a revolution, how the Jungian points of contact between Marcus Aurelius and Michelangelo's David were young beautiful boys and phenomenological criticism was the one ism that would drive a person insane if existentialism didn't first. Neither they nor I often knew what I was talking about, but they nodded and uh-huhed, then shuffled away. Once I caught Maria, the girl in the cubicle next to mine, repeating my drivel in the hallway. She knew I had caught her and so she called me over and said, What was it you were saying about Freud?

Freud was a devil worshipper. Everyone knows that. And watch out for the new historicists. They'll take up your life arguing the tensile strength of a poodle's vagina.

They thought I was being flip and witty and called me Dorothy Parker on crack. The meaner and crazier my words, the more they wanted to talk to me.

Maria and I started going out for happy hours and practicing what I called the Lacanian Deconstructionist Get. We waited for a mark, an unsuspecting actor or musician or broker or writer—young brokers were fun, strategic, they knew how to lie and sell themselves. They would tell us their stories then we would augment our stories with details to fit their stories and they would do the same until we'd broken each other down to a mutual relationship of perceived desires, which was never close. All I wanted was a book and glass of wine at the Neue Gallery. My alter ego liked sex on top of the Brooklyn Bridge.

Maria was an avid pupil, something of a superhero sidekick. She got all into it and gave us secret superhero names. Cherry Wollstonecraft and Justine Luscious. And she gave us an official mission statement: Usurping male libidos for the betterment of society through literary theory and sex. It was a nice idea. Made us sound legitimate but I wasn't in it for society. I couldn't have cared less about society. It was the role play.

Once I was a sex therapist. Once I was a fallen nun. Once I told a young square-jawed Wall Street man I'd only just, that day, come out of the closet. That I wasn't really lesbian and I'd never been fucked by a real penis and it was killing me. Then I told him I faked my homosexuality to get back at my parents for holding a trust fund over my head, that they had stipulated I must be married, to a man, in order to receive the money and so I'd never had sex because to keep up the act, I had to really play the part. Method acting like Pacino. Anything less wouldn't do. When Wall Street asked who my father was, I said I couldn't tell him, that I had been forbidden to discuss my father or his companies when out drinking with friends, that it was unsafe for me. He took me downtown, to the Meatpacking District, where he had a loft and a roll around wine cellar. It was a funny little thing. A temperature controlled box on wheels and he rolled it to the bed and set two wine glasses on the bed stand then started to list off the reds—Pinot Noir, Cabernet, a Bordeaux I knew to be cheap but one he seemed to be very proud of so I chose that one. After he came on my stomach, he went to the bathroom and grabbed a hand towel and cleaned me up with an awkward way that suggested he didn't often clean up his messes. He said, Are you okay? I said, Yeah, of course.

It's just . . . It's your first time.

I'm fine. It was an existential experience.

I'd like to see you again.

You don't even know me.

I feel like I do. It's weird. I feel like I know you.

Are you sure it isn't the billions? Or is it the virgin thing? I'm asking for purely academic reasons.

Billions?

Yeah, billions.

Wall Street texted me for weeks. It became a game. I kept spreadsheets and charts for how long men would text, unanswered, based upon the stories I told them. The ex-lesbian virgin heiress was my best seller.

Maria's game was simple. She would mark a Wall Street type and fuck him immediately. Sometimes in the bathroom of whatever restaurant or store or home we happened to be in. Then two weeks later she would call him and tell him she was pregnant, that the condom must have broken. She would cry and yell at him for buying cheap condoms. Then she would tell him she didn't have money for an abortion and if she could only get the money, she could go home to her grandmother's and have it taken care of. Maria had a ninety-six percent success rate. She sometimes worked two Wall Streets a week. I tried to tell her it was backwards prostitution. That she had turned into Lex Luthor. But she only laughed and said she was Robin Hood stealing from Wall Street to pay her rent.

I said, But Robin Hood gave to the poor. He didn't take it all for himself.

Then I'll donate a small portion to the local homeless shelter? Okay?

When Maria got pregnant for real, she retired from Justine Luscious and married the guy. They live in a duplex in Jersey now. Three kids. She sends me Christmas postcards with pictures of her kids on the front and her signature on the back. Justine with an x and an o.

I looked for another sidekick but never found another Justine Luscious. The closest I came was a doped up hooker in the subway. She fancied herself a trapeze artist and wanted to wear red and blue leotards and crawl across rooftops and call herself Spidercunt. I tried to explain how our mission wasn't really to be super heroes, that it was only a pretense. Eventually Spidercunt went her own way and got an agent, an old pimp named Charlie. He sold the rights to her book, *Spidercunt Saves the World*. Random House paid for a book tour. Pacino bought the movie rights. *Spidercunt* releases next spring.

From time to time, I look back at Cherry Wollstonecraft and Justine Luscious' spreadsheets and dream a little dream and I imagine, somewhere, somehow, we made a difference. That even if we hadn't saved the world, we'd thrown a few Wall Streets off course. And days when I sit in my little cubicle wondering what the hell I've done with my life, Cherry Wollstonecraft and Justine Luscious still make me smile. I pack up my desk, turn off the light, head out into the Manhattan air and find a quiet place at a quiet bar and if a man sits beside me, offers to buy me a drink, I listen to his story.

UNKNOWN PLEASURES
BY JEB GLEASON-ALLURED

She's been following me since at least 29th Street, a rapid clipping of heels trailing close along whole blocks of walled-off construction, past a window filled with Porches and another filled with Bentleys, past buildings swallowed up in shadow.

"Excuse me," the woman calls, in a high, faltering voice. "Excuse me, but I think you're wearing my hat. That's my hat."

At 24th Street I cut east and pick up speed, blurring past galleries and passing under the Highline overpass where the sunset winks off tourists' cameras.

"Excuse me, Miss," the woman says. "You're wearing my hat. That's my hat."

I don't turn to look, but at the next corner I catch a flash of her in the window of the cab parked at the Lukoil—magenta tights, gush of blond hair. I pinch the front brim of the boater between thumb and forefinger and duck my head into a blast of autumn wind. A delivery truck just misses me crossing Tenth Avenue—"Lady, what the fuck!"—and then I am hustling along a quiet, leafy block, side-stepping smears of dog shit. Beneath my trench coat I'm filmed with sweat, my breath growing shallow, a panicked numbness seeping up my thighs.

"Miss, you're wearing my hat."

She's right behind me again. People are looking at us oddly as we pass. Not looking like they are going to intervene, just watching the solemn spectacle of one woman pursuing another in the twilight.

"Miss, you're wearing my hat."

"I think you're mistaken," I say into the wind.

She is not mistaken. It is her hat. I stole it. I steal lots of things. Not from department stores or boutiques. Mostly from parties. Rooftop cocktails in Hell's Kitchen, backyard barbecues in Bushwick, potlucks in Astoria. I raid closets, dressers, hampers, bedroom floors, plucking anything that stirs me, that feels lived in, that carries the mark of the owner. My closets are filled with all kinds of plunder—a red kimono swarming with birds, a disintegrating t-shirt reeking of underarms, gray plimsoles sugared with the sand of some unknown beach (worn out the door by me in full view of the hostess).

Why do I steal? What do I do with the things I steal? These are the things people ask me when I confess. I only confess to someone I'm going to know the rest of my life (my brother Ray) or someone I will never see again (the guy who picked me up at a friend's gallery opening last week). After some slow, weird sex, he sat smoking and smiling on my bed, jaw propped on his fist as I ran through the possible motives. I'm a sociopath, I crave a connection, I want to inhabit the being of another, like cavemen did with pelts. I steal from men, women—an androgynous thief.

Sometimes I'll put on a fashion show for the person I will never see again, their eyes following me as I disappear and emerge, disappear and emerge from the tiny tiled bathroom. Are you going to steal something from me, they'll say, and I'll say don't be so arrogant. And then maybe we'll fuck again or they'll leave and either way they're usually one article of clothing lighter.

The first thing I ever stole was Ray's stretched out Joy Division shirt, the one with the mountain range of pulsing frequency lines from the *Unknown Pleasures* album. It had the smell of cigarettes and the ghost of some girl's fruity perfume. I was maybe 13, I had green hair. He wasn't going to need it in Kabul or Kunduz or wherever the fuck he was being sent. Just before he headed back to Fort Benning for the last time, Ray stood in my doorway, scratching his prickly scalp and asking if I'd seen the shirt. No, I said, looking at the furrow between his big black eyes. I hadn't seen it.

After Ray had left, becoming just a string of brief emails sent from a series of forward operating bases "somewhere in The Big A," we read the abridged *Odyssey* in class, about the robe Penelope never stopped weaving while Odysseus was on his journey home from Troy. I started wearing the Joy Division shirt every day, until I was called into the school counselor's office and was told "there have been some concerns."

At Eighth Avenue I turn south. The pocket of my trench coat vibrates. I pull out the phone. Chicago area code. Three bounced calls from Ray's girlfriend, what's her name. The born-again babe with the poodle hair. And two texts—some Bible verse about putting wrath and anger and malice away, and then a scarier one saying only *he's worse you have to call.* I put the phone away. At 23rd Street I duck down the subway steps. I can hear the woman's voice echoing after me—"Miss, please stop, that's my hat, I need my hat"—as I fumble for and then swipe my Metrocard, then slip sideways between the closing doors of a downtown E train. I clutch the center pole, stare at my reflection in one of the windows. Tentacles of sweat-slicked hair reach across my forehead. The boater, the trench coat, the pink shirtdress. Disjointed pieces of other people. I look like I was dressed by some demented committee.

The train scrapes and screeches through the darkness beneath the city. At 14th Street it stops and stays stopped. After a moment, the loudspeaker crackles. "Ladies and gentlemen, due to a police investigation at the next station this will be our last stop, our last stop." Everyone shuffles off the train, looking around the grimy platform, trying to figure out what to do next. "Police investigation means someone jumped in front of a train," one girl tells another girl. "It's, like, code." I remember when Ray's last girlfriend, the pretty one with the bad teeth, called my parents to say he'd had an "episode" after his last deployment, which turned out to be code for two slashed wrists and one mini-van driven into a neighbor's house.

I jog up one flight of steps and down another to the L. Station after station, the car fills up with more and more people, then suddenly releases most of them on the far side of the East River. The whole time I focus on the floor between my ballet flats. Black linoleum flecked with red and white, like deep space. Suddenly I become aware of something. A vibration in my periphery. Slouchy boots. Magenta tights. I can't raise my eyes.

"Please," she says. "All I want is my hat back. Please don't make me keep chasing you."

My eyes drift up, across the ruffles of her baggy white dress, the chunky blue necklace, the face, the face, the face, the cable-knit beret like her own personal raincloud. I remember her immediately as the hostess of a party, maybe a year or so back, a smiling, pretty woman with a hand clapped perpetually to her protruding belly. I'd been dating

21

Dasim then, who I think was a friend or a friend of a friend of the father to be. I don't remember what the occasion was, or who we talked to or about what, but I remember how happy the woman had been, drifting from person to person, answering questions about baby names, due dates. I'd found the boater on a hook in the spare room where the coats were piled on a bed. It had a navy blue band with a green stripe through the middle and a straw brim darkened from decades of handling. The inside smelled of sweat and a woman's shampoo. I had slipped it under my jacket, which I carried over one arm as we left. When Dasim broke up with me a month or so later he told me no one could ever love me enough.

"How is the baby," I say, and then clarify for some reason, "how is *your* baby?"

"What?" she says, obviously not recognizing me from the party.

She shakes her head side to side until the confusion clears from it.

"It belonged to my grandfather," she says. "His second wife got everything when he died and she hated us, his original family. This is all I got after the funeral."

The train lurches. Tinny music leeches from a boy's ear buds. The woman extracts a phone from the WNYC tote bag on her shoulder. She punches in a code, swipes through several screens, holds the phone's face to my face. He poses in the grainy-bleachy light, a spindly little thing in a baggy suit, grass up to his knees, a tiny farm house floating on the horizon line. The boater is tipped back from his big round face, a distant echo of the woman holding the phone. He smiles embarrassedly at the photographer, whose shadow reaches toward him.

"Thank you," she says, when I hand her the hat.

22

I get off at the next stop. She doesn't. I climb the stairs of the unfamiliar station, wind blasting down at me from street level. Fading blue sky above black buildings. I stand on the corner, not sure which direction is which, exactly. I pull out my phone, press my brother's number with my thumb . . . wait for what happens next.

IF YOU CAN'T STAND THE HEAT
BY LAWRENCE BLOCK

She felt his eyes on her just about the time the bartender placed a Beck's coaster on the bar and set her dry Rob Roy on top of it. She wanted to turn and see who was eyeing her, but remained as she was, trying to analyze just what it was she felt. She couldn't pin it down physically, couldn't detect a specific prickling of the nerves in the back of her neck. She simply knew she was being watched, and that the watcher was a male.

It was, to be sure, a familiar sensation. Men had always looked at her. Since adolescence, since her body had begun the transformation from girl to woman? No, longer than that. Even in childhood, some men had looked at her, gazing with admiration and, often, with something beyond admiration.

In Hawley, Minnesota, thirty miles east of the North Dakota line, they'd looked at her like that. The glances followed her to Red Cloud and St. Paul, and other places after that, and now she was in New York, and, no surprise, men still looked at her.

She lifted her glass, sipped, and a male voice said, "Excuse me, but is that a Rob Roy?"

He was standing to her left, a tall man, slender, well turned out in a navy blazer and gray trousers. His shirt was a button-down, his tie diagonally striped. His face, attractive but not handsome, was youthful at first glance, but she could see he'd lived some lines into it. And his dark hair was lightly infiltrated with gray.

"A dry Rob Roy," she said. "Why?"

"In a world where everyone orders Cosmopolitans," he said, "there's something very pleasingly old-fashioned about a girl who drinks a Rob Roy. A woman, I should say."

She lowered her eyes to see what he was drinking.

"I haven't ordered yet," he said. "Just got here. I'd have one of those, but old habits die hard." And, when the barman moved in front of him, he ordered Jameson on the rocks. "Irish whiskey," he told her. "Of course this neighborhood used to be mostly Irish. And tough. It was a pretty dangerous place a few years ago. A young woman like yourself wouldn't feel comfortable walking into a bar unaccompanied, not in this part of town. Even accompanied, it was no place for a lady."

"I guess it's changed a lot," she said.

"It's even changed its name," he said. His drink arrived, and he picked up his glass and held it to the light, admiring the amber color. "They call it Clinton now. That's for DeWitt Clinton, not Bill. DeWitt was the governor a while back, he dug the Erie Canal. Not personally, but he got it done. And there was George Clinton, he was the governor, too, for seven terms starting before the adoption of the Constitution. And then he had a term as vice president. But all that was before your time."

"By a few years," she allowed.

"It was even before mine," he said. "But I grew up here, just a few blocks from here, and I can tell you nobody called it Clinton then. You probably know what they called it."

"Hell's Kitchen," she said. "They still call it that, when they're not calling it Clinton."

"Well, it's more colorful. It was the real estate interests who plumped for Clinton, because they figured nobody would want to move to something called Hell's Kitchen. And that may have been true then, when people remembered what a bad neighborhood this was, but now it's spruced up and gentrified and yuppified to within an inch of its life, and the old name gives it a little added cachet. A touch of gangster chic, if you know what I mean."

"If you can't stand the heat—"

"Stay out of the Kitchen," he supplied. "When I was growing up here, the Westies pretty much ran the place. They weren't terribly efficient, like the Italian mob, but they were colorful and bloodthirsty enough to make up for it. There was a man two doors down the street from me who disappeared, and they never did find the body. Except one of his hands turned up in somebody's freezer on 53rd Street and Eleventh Avenue. They wanted to be able to put his fingerprints on things long after he was dead and gone."

"Would that work?"

"With luck," he said, "we'll never know. The Westies are mostly gone now, and the tenement apartments they lived in are all tarted up, with stockbrokers and lawyers renting them now. Which are you?"

"Me?"

"A stockbroker? Or a lawyer?"

She grinned. "Neither one, I'm afraid. I'm an actress."

"Even better."

"Which means I take a class twice a week," she said, "and run around to open casting calls and auditions."

"And wait tables?"

"I did some of that in the Cities. I suppose I'll have to do it again here, when I start to run out of money."

"The Cities?"

"The Twin Cities. Minneapolis and St. Paul."

"That's where you're from?"

They talked about where she was from, and along the way he told her his name was Jim. She was Jennifer, she told him. He related another story about the neighborhood—he was really a pretty good storyteller—and by then her Rob Roy was gone and so was his Jameson. "Let me get us another round," he said, "and then why don't we take our drinks to a table? We'll be more comfortable, and it'll be quieter."

He was talking about the neighborhood.

"Irish, of course," he said, "but that was only part of it. You had blocks that were pretty much solid Italian, and there were Poles and other Eastern Europeans. A lot of French, too, working at the restaurants in the theater district. You had everything, really. The UN's across town on the East River, but you had your own General Assembly here in the Kitchen. Fifty-seventh Street was a dividing line; north of that was San Juan Hill, and you had a lot of blacks living there. It was an interesting place to grow up, if you got to grow up, but no sweet young thing from Minnesota would want to move here."

She raised her eyebrows at *sweet young thing*, and he grinned at her. Then his eyes turned serious and he said, "I have a confession to make."

"Oh?"

"I followed you in here."

"You mean you noticed me even before I ordered a Rob Roy?"

"I saw you on the street. And for a moment I thought—"

"What?"

"Well, that you were on the street."

"I guess I was, if that's where you saw me. I don't…oh, you thought—"

"That you were a working girl. I wasn't going to mention this, and I don't want you to take it the wrong way—"

What, she wondered, was the right way?

"—because it's not as though you looked the part, or were dressed like the girls you see out there. See, the neighborhood may be tarted up, but that doesn't mean the tarts have disappeared."

"I've noticed."

"It was more the way you were walking," he went on. "Not swinging your hips, not your walk per se, but a feeling I got that you weren't in a hurry to get anywhere, or even all that sure where you were going."

"I was thinking about stopping for a drink," she said, "and not sure if I wanted to, or if I should go straight home."

"That would fit."

"And I've never been in here before, and wondered if it was decent."

"Well, it's decent enough now. A few years ago it wouldn't have been. And even now, a woman alone—"

"I see." She sipped her drink. "So you thought I might be a hooker," she said, "and that's what brought you in here. Well, I hate to disappoint you—"

"What brought me in here," he said, "was the thought that you might be, and the hope that you weren't."

"I'm not."

"I know."

"I'm an actress."

"And a good one, I'll bet."

"I guess time will tell."

"It generally does," he said. "Can I get you another one of those?"

She shook her head. "Oh, I don't think so," she said. "I was only going to come in for one drink, and I wasn't even sure I wanted to do that. And I've had two, and that's really plenty."

"Are you sure?"

"I'm afraid so. It's not just the alcohol, it's the time. I have to get home."

"I'll walk you."

"Oh, that's not necessary."

"Yes, it is. Whether it's Hell's Kitchen or Clinton, it's still necessary."

"Well . . ."

"I insist. It's safer around here than it used to be, but it's a long way from Minnesota. And I suppose you get some unsavory characters in Minnesota, as far as that goes."

"Well, you're right about that," she said. And at the door she said, "I just don't want you to think you have to walk me home because I'm a lady."

"I'm not walking you home because you're a lady," he said. "I'm walking you home because I'm a gentleman."

The walk to her door was interesting. He had stories to tell about half the buildings they passed. There'd been a murder in this one, a notorious drunk in the next. For all that some of the stories were unsettling, she felt completely secure walking at his side.

At her door he said, "Any chance I could come up for a cup of coffee?"

"I wish," she said.

"I see."

"I've got this roommate," she said. "It's impossible, it really is. My idea of success isn't starring on Broadway, it's making enough money to have a place of my own. There's just no privacy when she's home, and the damn girl is always home."

"That's a shame."

She drew a breath. "Jim? Do you have a roommate?"

He didn't, and if he had the place would still have been large enough to afford privacy. A large living room, a big bedroom, a good-sized kitchen. Rent-controlled, he told her, or he could never have afforded it. He showed her all through the apartment before he took her in his arms and kissed her.

"Maybe," she said, when the embrace ended, "maybe we should have one more drink after all."

She was dreaming, something confused and confusing, and then her eyes snapped open. For a moment she did not know where she was, and then she realized she was in New York, and realized the dream had been a recollection or reinvention of her childhood in Hawley.

In New York, and in Jim's apartment.

And in his bed. She turned, saw him lying motionless beside her, and slipped out from under the covers, moving with instinctive caution. She walked quietly out of the bedroom, found the bathroom. She used the toilet, peeked behind the shower curtain. The tub was surprisingly clean for a bachelor's apartment, and looked inviting. She didn't feel soiled, not exactly that, but something close. Stale, she decided. Stale, and very much in need of freshening.

She ran the shower, adjusted the temperature, stepped under the spray.

She hadn't intended to stay over, had fallen asleep in spite of her intentions. Rohypnol, she thought. Roofies, the date-rape drug. Puts you to sleep, or the closest thing to it, and leaves you with no memory of what happened to you.

Maybe that was it. Maybe she'd gotten a contact high.

She stepped out of the tub, toweled herself dry, and returned to the bedroom for her clothes. He hadn't moved in her absence and lay on his back beneath the covers.

She got dressed, checked herself in the mirror, found her purse, put on lipstick but no makeup, and was satisfied with the results. Then, after another reflexive glance at the bed, she began searching the apartment.

His wallet, in the gray slacks he'd tossed over the back of a chair, held almost three hundred dollars in cash. She took that but left the credit cards and everything else. She found just over a thousand dollars in his sock drawer, and took it, but left the mayonnaise jar full of loose change. She checked the refrigerator, and the set of brushed aluminum containers on the kitchen counter, but the fridge held nothing but food and drink, and one container held tea bags while the other two were empty.

That was probably it, she decided. She could search more thoroughly, but she'd only be wasting her time.

And she really ought to get out of here.

But first she had to go back to the bedroom. Had to stand at the side of the bed and look down at him. Jim, he'd called himself. James John O'Rourke, according to the cards in his wallet. Forty-seven years old. Old enough to be her father, in point of fact, although the man in Hawley who'd sired her was his senior by eight or nine years.

He hadn't moved.

Rohypnol, she thought. The love pill.

"Maybe," she had said, "we should have one more drink after all."

I'll have what you're having, she'd told him, and it was child's play to add the drug to her own drink, then switch glasses with him. Her only concern after that had been that he might pass out before he got his clothes off, but no, they kissed and petted and found their way to his bed, and got out of their clothes and into each other's arms, and it was all very nice, actually, until he yawned and his muscles went slack and he lay limp in her arms.

She arranged him on him on his back and watched him sleep. Then she touched and stroked him, eliciting a response without waking the sleeping giant. Rohypnol, the wonder drug, facilitating date rape for either sex. She took him in her mouth, she mounted him, she rode him. Her orgasm was intense, and it was hers alone. He didn't share it, and when she dismounted his penis softened and lay upon his thigh.

In Hawley her father took to coming into her room at night. "Kitten? Are you sleeping?" If she answered, he'd kiss her on the forehead and tell her to go back to sleep.

Then half an hour later he'd come back. If she was asleep, if she didn't hear him call her name, he'd slip into the bed with her. And touch her, and kiss her, and not on her forehead this time.

She would wake up when this happened, but somehow knew to feign sleep. And he would do what he did.

Before long she pretended to be asleep whenever he came into the room. She'd hear him ask if she was asleep, and she'd lie there silent and still, and he'd come into her bed. She liked it, she didn't like it. She loved him, she hated him.

Eventually they dropped the pretense. Eventually he taught her how to touch him, and how to use her mouth on him. Eventually, eventually, there was very little they didn't do.

It took some work, but she got Jim hard again, and this time she made him come. He moaned audibly at the very end, then subsided into deep sleep almost immediately. She was exhausted, she felt as if she'd taken a drug herself, but she forced herself to go to the bathroom and look for some Listerine. She couldn't find any, and wound up gargling with a mouthful of his Irish whiskey.

She stopped in the kitchen, then returned to the bedroom. And, when she'd done what she needed to do, she decided it wouldn't hurt to lie down beside him and close her eyes. Just for a minute . . .

And now it was morning, and time for her to get out of there. She stood looking down at him, and for an instant she seemed to see his chest rise and fall with his slow even breathing, but that was just her mind playing a trick, because his chest was in fact quite motionless, and he wasn't breathing at all. His breathing had stopped forever when she slid the kitchen knife between two of his ribs and into his heart.

He'd died without a sound. *La petite mort,* the French called orgasm. The little death. Well, the little death had drawn a moan from him, but the real thing turned out to be soundless. His breathing stopped, and never resumed.

She laid a hand on his upper arm, and the coolness of his flesh struck her as a sign that he was at peace now. She thought, almost wistfully, how very serene he had become.

In a sense, there'd been no need to kill the man. She could have robbed him just as effectively while he slept, and the drug would ensure that he wouldn't wake up before she was out the door. She'd used the knife in response to an inner need, and the need had in fact been an urgent one; satisfying it had shuttled her right off to sleep.

Back in Hawley, her mother's kitchen had held every kind of knife you could imagine. A dozen of them jutted out of a butcher-block knife holder, and others filled a shallow drawer. Sometimes she'd look at the knives, and think about them, and the things you could do with them. Cutting, piercing. Knife-type things.

"You're my little soldier," her father used to say, and she felt like a soldier the night of her high school graduation, marching when her name was called, standing at attention to receive her diploma. She could feel the buzz in the audience, men and women telling each other how brave she was. The poor child, with all she'd been through.

She never touched her mother's knives, and for all she knew they were still in the kitchen in Hawley. But a few weeks later she left her apartment in St. Paul and went bar-hopping across the river in Minneapolis, and the young man she went home with had a set of knives in a butcher-block holder, just like her mother's.

Bad luck for him.

She let herself out of the apartment, drew the door shut and made sure it locked behind her. The building was a walk-up, four apartments to the floor, and she made her way down three flights and out the door without encountering anyone.

Time to think about moving.

Not that she'd established a pattern. The man last week, in the posh loft near the Javits Center, had smothered to death. He'd been huge, and built like a wrestler, but the drug rendered him helpless, and all she'd had to do was hold the pillow over his face. He didn't come close enough to consciousness to struggle. And the man before that, the advertising executive, had shown her why he'd feel safe in any neighborhood, gentrification or no. He kept a loaded handgun in the drawer of the bedside table, and if any burglar was unlucky enough to drop into his place, well—

When she was through with him, she'd retrieved the gun, wrapped his hand around it, put the barrel in his mouth, and squeezed off a shot. They could call it a suicide, even as they could call the wrestler a heart attack, if they didn't look too closely. Or they could call all three of them murders without ever suspecting they were all the work of the same person.

Still, it wouldn't hurt her to move. Find another place to live before people started to notice her on the streets and in the bars. She liked it here, in Clinton or Hell's Kitchen, whatever you wanted to call it. It was a nice place to live, whatever it may have been in years past. But, as she and Jim had agreed, the whole of Manhattan was a nice place to live. There weren't any bad neighborhoods left, not really.

Wherever she went, she was pretty sure she'd feel safe.

NEGATIVE SPACE
BY SION DAYSON

The expectation as I mapped out the day was that I'd be standing naked for a good portion of it. This turned out not to be the case; obviously something had to give. I'd showed up at the Art Institute and I suppose that was the test. The professor who'd placed the ad—"models for art class"—showed me examples of life drawings and the corresponding negative space, what I was to do. Sure, *strangers with sharpened pencils.*

Instead here I am, fully clothed. Hot. Purposeless.

I'm downtown and could be anywhere with a few steps. Pick a direction. [Forward]. Soho, Chinatown, the Village, melting into each other as we melt. *Is the rain coming back?.* Days like these—the summer ones, the no-place-to-be ones, I'm-unemployed-and-young ones—these are the best for getting back in touch with self-reliance. I have no sense of direction.

I begin one of my aimless walks around my New York. This is how I'd first come to know her—wandering unfamiliar streets as if they were nameless country roads. Walked till my feet ached and I was lost, no choice but to find my way home. *I am of uptown.*

It's the sticky sweat after a humid city rain, the heat, concretized, angles between skyscrapers and corner bodegas. I pass an outdoor terrace. *Oh, I drank lemonade there with Noah. Noah is gone—I cannot drink lemonade with Noah anymore.* I hear avant-garde jazz near the federal courthouse. The Knitting Factory's so close. I didn't realize . . . that . . . *Parallel no longer runs straight.*

Open to a plaza. A homeless man is raptly reading the newspaper. I try not to stare at his dreadlocked hair. It is of such a length—and such a stiffness—good lord, those dirty socks. Which paper is he reading? The fucking *Post,* man? You've got to be joking.

Three sirens are nothing new in any part of the city I know. Of course, I don't hang around the Upper East Side. I'm not Murray Hill or Wall Street. I once partied in a Gramercy Park penthouse, but the circumstances were "extenuating." No, *I am of uptown.* Three police cars pass, no cause for alarm. I cross over Lafayette Street. J-M-Z. The subway is a big deal to me. 4-5-6.

But I'm not here to discuss that matter. I'm trying to tell you about the three police cars that turned into dozens. That kept streaming by. That surround-sounded the plaza.

This is no joke, life is one big circle, a series of circles. I'm sure I read that in some Eastern philosophy book. *Chinatown.* I see the interlocking red circle sculpture behind City Hall. Two days ago I stood at that sculpture and took wedding pictures. *Not my own.* My friend was wearing a funky white vintage dress and two-dollar Salvation Army shoes. Her beau (she won't let me say husband even though he is now) wore a nice white shirt and jeans. Sneakers. I wore a plastered smile. The whole thing was weird.

So I had circled back to the red circle statue after two days. The sirens have multiplied now, screaming consistent, insistent alerts. Unmarked cars with sirens, too. Why did I circle back to this place? *I am of uptown.* Police cars are now coming from all directions. Down Centre, still on Lafayette, Chambers, off the Brooklyn Bridge, through the park. That is not a street, but they are coming from the park.

I am in New York. A double-decker sightseeing bus is turning the corner onto Chambers. *Cause for alarm, unmarked cars.* The tourists on top are standing up, agitated. Or excited. Or both. They all take pictures. They will return to Kansas and say *"Yes, and a hundred police cars circle City Hall there—just like TV."* Law and order.

I am not anxious. Just *oh no, not again.* I stand transfixed by the surround-sound sirens, the cops lining the block. Four men sprint down Centre and ark left into the building. They are plainclothes men, but I see a gun. Real civilians don't run like that. At least I don't think they do. I have not been a civilian who runs like that. Two towers fell.

The sky is deciding whether it wants to return to rain. The drizzle does not dampen the surround sound sirens down. A man is walking past me. *Hello. Hello.* It sometimes means too much to acknowledge someone else's existence in New York. *I am in New York.* So he stops. *I want to know what is going on before I get on the train.* I agree. *I am of uptown. "Just like one of those episodes."* Law and order. City hall crime doesn't happen in Harlem. Harlem crime happens in Harlem. *Oh no, not again.* Even a terrorist must know you don't have to hurt the black folks for show.

The A express is the best. *Yeah, it's safer in Harlem. I need someone to ride home with me. I'm scared. Are you scared?* I am not scared. This man is not scared. He was headed toward the 4-5-6 before he stopped. East Harlem. I am West Harlem. He is December. I am May.

Someone got shot. East December is trying to talk to me. There is now a steady stream, a steady scream of police vehicles coming down Chambers. And East December is trying to talk to me. *I'm going to call my friend at the Fire Department—they always know what's going on.* Jason. Here I am marveling that East December, at a time like this [uncertain danger], is trying to pick up a pretty little thing.

But then, here I am calling Jason. He is not in the firehouse. And I am thinking about him at a time like this [possible tragedy]. *Do you have a boyfriend,* East December asks. *Yes.* Jason. Jason is not my boyfriend. But at a time like this [*extenuating* circumstances], I am thinking that he once was. At a time like this [often], I am thinking that way. December talks to May.

Shopkeepers come out from their stores. It's raining again, but I want to stay to find out why sirens are screaming. *This is too serious for just someone getting shot.* December. I cannot move. We stay in New York. *I'm at the World Trade Center wearing a kufi on my head—I'm in more danger than you, sister.*

I am of uptown, better get to Harlem.

There is a study group that meets on Thursdays. Are you interested in culture?

African culture. We study.

I take out my notebook. Calvin Cain writes down his name. And every which way to reach him.

And your number?

I'm not giving you my number.

Boyfriend? Two? Six? You are so beautiful. If I could just be half of one.

I am of uptown, I'd better get home.

How will I know if you get home safe? Just a cell phone number so I know that you're safe. You won't know if I'm safe. You don't care?

We stay in New York. Surround sound sirens down. Two towers fell. Still, everything could collapse and December will always try for May. Cops are everywhere, trains sequestered. *But I am of uptown, I must get to Harlem.* And the A train, it's the best. *There's some real shit going on.* I descend underground. No one is nervous. It is New York. We stay. *Someone got shot, that's what I heard.*

The A train's not running . . . and then it is. It takes me all the way. 125th and there's a call that I missed. Jason, at this time [now], though I had promised myself this time [before now] I would not talk to him. Jason is not my boyfriend. At a time like this [life].

A councilman was shot six times. You knew before us.

Ah! Knew before them. I know that I am in New York. I turn on my computer at a time like this [confusion]. I see on the Internet where I just was, all of the riot gear, a stretcher. Oh, so things are real even before reporters get there. I forget that about the news. You can be there [New York] before it's news. It is new. I am May writing circumstances sharpened forward. Today I talked briefly of negative space.

BAD KARMA
BY RON KOLM

It was hazy, hot and humid. Gritty summer air banged down on the tarpaper roof of the abandoned building on Avenue C where Duke and Jill lived, bringing it to a slow boil. Duke was crouched in a corner of their room, surrounded by stacks of porno mags, water-damaged books, battered 1940s-style table fans and heaps of women's clothing.

"Watcha doin,' honey?" Jill asked him.

"Taking inventory," he growled back. Duke was in a bad mood. The heat was making him sweat heavily, and drops of it were falling onto his best magazines—the ones he'd managed to keep in mint condition despite the daily grind of trying to sell them on the street.

"Fucking shit!" Duke fumed, wiping his face with a lacy pink camisole. The effort made him sweat even more. "Damn it, Jill, our stock's running really low—we don't have enough good stuff left to get us more than a six-pack or two, and maybe a nickel bag."

"I get the message," Jill yelled from the sweltering bathroom. She was trying to mousse her grown-out shag into a bouffant. "You want me to go out and cop some merchandise."

"Yeah," Duke said. "What I really need are more 'zines— these are getting too fucking beat up."

Jill rummaged through the piles of dirty clothing for a pair of large-waisted jeans with sharply tapered legs. She also put on a loose black T-shirt and left it untucked.

"You know how much I hate doing this," she said to Duke. She chugged down a couple of beers. Then she did a few lines to give her an edge and left the tiny hot apartment.

The streets were steaming.

Jill checked out Gem Spa and the other neighborhood newsstands, but they were all on to her. With "get the fuck oudda here, ya thief" still ringing in her ears, Jill sat down on the curb and popped some pills to help her think. Unfortunately, the only idea she could come up with was to 'borrow' some product from another peddler.

Jill lurched over to the large black cube sculpture at the triangular intersection of Fourth Avenue and Lafayette Street. A bunch of street peddlers were set up there, displaying their wares in the shadow of the cube. One guy was selling bootleg Dead tapes, another featured several plastic milk crates filled with badly scratched jazz LPs.

Jill felt dizzy. The heat seemed to be magnifying the effects of the pills as she scanned the various items for sale. She leaned on the sculpture for support. And then, swimming into focus, there they were—row upon row of vintage soft-core porn magazines—*Swank*, *Genesis*, *Penthouse*, *High Society*, *Hustler* and yes, a 1953 *Playboy*—all of them in perfect condition. Just what Duke wanted.

Jill got it together and approached the sun-baked, pot-bellied man who sat smiling amid them. He was wearing only a tattered pair of cutoffs and his bald head gleamed in the sun.

"Can you tell me where St. Mark's Place is?" she slurred.

The man looked beatifically into her wildly gyrating green eyes. As he turned to point out directions she scooped up an armful of magazines, slid them under her shirt and skillfully tucked them into the top of her jeans in one fluid motion. And that's when the heat, the beers and the drugs hit her full force. She fell face down on the concrete.

At that exact moment Duke showed up – he'd gone out to score some stuff on his own. He sprinted over to Jill, rolled her onto her back and put his head against her chest to check for a heartbeat. As he did so, the spine of a porno mag poked him in the eye through her T-shirt. Thinking quickly, Duke hoisted Jill up by the armpits and draped her over his shoulder in such a way as to keep the stolen booty from shaking loose and falling out.

"Hey, man," Duke said to the peddler, "too much to drink—happens all the time—I'll see that she gets home okay." Duke grinned at the man in fraternal understanding and then staggered off under the dead weight of Jill's limp body.

Darkness brought no relief—if anything, the humidity seemed to increase, and a thick dirty fog settled over the Lower East Side.

Duke arranged his display of girlie magazines on a flattened piece of cardboard in front of 'Love Saves the Day,' the hip chotchke shop on the corner of 7th Street and Second Avenue. He carefully positioned his newest treasure, the 1953 *Playboy*, in the center of it. Jill had scored really big this time. He'd carried her all the way back to their joint, his tank top rank with sweat. After dragging her up five flights of stairs and into their room, he was finally able to revive her using the ancient secrets of drug culture medical lore.

Duke snapped back to reality—a guy was picking up his centerpiece and thumbing through the pages. Duke checked him out. He was a large, muscular white guy, dressed all in black; black pants, black leather jacket and black motorcycle boots. Guy must be crazy, Duke thought, it's still fuckin' 90 degrees! The guy's greasy 50s-style pompadour contrasted sharply with Duke's stringy shoulder-length locks.

The guy casually rolled up the *Playboy*, jammed it in his jacket pocket and turned away, walking north towards St. Marks Place.

"Hey, fucking shit, man – that's my merchandise!" Duke yelled. "Ya gotta *pay* for it if you want it!" The guy didn't stop. "Hey, man, watch my stuff – I'll be right back," Duke said to the peddler selling next to him. He jumped up and ran after the guy, who made no attempt to get away.

The big guy walked nonchalantly up Second Avenue, seemingly oblivious to Duke's shouting and cursing. He turned east, crossing the avenue at 9th Street, and Duke followed. He was livid with anger, but he didn't know what to do. The guy was *way* too big to attack—Duke was a skinny five-foot-six, even Jill towered over him— he didn't really want to die over a magazine—and he couldn't very well call for the cops—they'd probably bust *him,* too.

As they neared the middle of the block the guy whirled around, his jacket fanning out, and he whipped his hand towards Duke as if he had a weapon in it. Duke jumped back, startled. But the guy merely gave him a weird smile and continued along 9th Street to First Avenue.

Duke was perplexed, and more than a little shaken up, but he stayed right on the guy's tail – just far enough back to run if the guy tried to charge him again.

They reached First Avenue, crossed it, and turned uptown towards 10th Street. And it was at that corner, in front of a neighborhood bodega, where the big guy made his final move. He stopped abruptly, picked up a heavy steel trash basket filled with garbage and heaved it at Duke. Duke just barely managed to avoid it. At that moment he noticed a long line of large green trash bags on the sidewalk, and a tiredness filled him as he pictured himself having to dodge each and every one of them.

The guy came at Duke shouting, "What do you want from me, faggot? You want to suck my ass? Is that it, faggot, you want to suck my ass?"

Duke looked around in desperation for any kind of weapon—and saw what appeared to be a stick protruding from one of the garbage bags. Duke pulled it out and was surprised to find himself holding a four-foot long broken fluorescent light tube with a jagged end. Fucking shit, I'm Obi-wan Kenobi, he thought.

"Yo, my man, don't hit him with that thing," someone said, "You'll get little slivers of glass in our eyes."

Duke looked over and saw a giant black dude with sweat bands on his wrists. And then it hit Duke—this was a drug corner, and that dude was the Main Man—and he and his new 'friend' were disturbing the evening's commerce—their fracas might even bring the cops crashing down—and the black dude obviously didn't want that to happen.

"S'up, my man," the Dealer asked Duke.

"Hey, man, I sell on the street, just like you, and that guy took something that belongs to me," he answered.

"Give it up," the black dude ordered the white guy, which he quickly did, meekly handing the *Playboy* to the Dealer, who, in turn, passed it on to Duke. "Now you go back to your spot and be cool with the tube—you don't want to be getting little slivers of glass in your eyes." And he flashed Duke the peace sign.

Under a streetlight on 9th Street Duke looked down at the cover of the *Playboy*, savoring the sexy pose of the girl who adorned it. She was once again his. But, damn, several droplets of water stitched a pattern across her body. Was his sweat ruining yet another magazine? Duke wiped his forehead with the back of his free hand—and it was then that he heard a long dull rumble of violent summer thunder.

Duke looked up just as the heavens opened.

MOMMA'S BOYS DON'T DO WELL IN THE GHETTO

BY KOFI FORSON

My roommate former professional basketball player in Denmark used to sit with me over vodka cocktails tell stories about how he got loaded on cocaine fucked cheerleaders one after the other. He was well respected by those who knew him, merchants who sold on the streets, stretching out east to west. Further north it got busier with peddlers, sidewalk traffic, fast food restaurants, out of date department stores. On Sundays when the sun hit that particular spark in the sky we headed out.

For lunch we had bodega specials, rice and beans with yucca sometimes bacalao. Sat across from him by a wooden dining table took serving of what we had, ate quietly listening to noise outside coming in, construction workers creating disturbance, children running up and down screaming, occasional car honking its horn and men standing out in front speaking Spanish. He would often ask about details in my schedule. I would always give him the basics. Whether I had slept with a woman on Park Avenue gotten over on some money or helped move furniture for an executive in the art world.

He imported items from places like Italy sold them secondhand on the streets, perfumes, fur coats, women's wear. On a trip out of town he left behind boxes of perfume. The apartment close to size and shape of a loft was full of these boxes. Before he left he had introduced me to most of the men he dealt with on regular basis. Experienced men having served time or not, they seemed ruthless. He brought me out like sacrificial lamb while one after the other the men smiled, their teeth yellow and decayed.

The apartment felt haunted. I awoke to the phone ringing over and over. Began squirming on the bed. Started to feel uneasy. Constant ringing was threatening to the point I sensed danger. On the recording a henchman explained how there had been a misunderstanding. He claimed the boxes were his took time explaining when he could come over. It wasn't so much anger I sensed. Listening on I got the idea he meant what he was saying. But he sounded desperate and that scared me.

Following morning I took off, spent a few days at my mothers. I walked in there faint, spineless and out of breath. Mother wasn't so much worried as she looked me over and never gave a damn. She went through routine of cleaning a dishpan, opening and closing the refrigerator, washing dishes. She had grown tired of me. One morning while I slept on the living room sofa she burst in told me to get the hell back to the apartment.

My roommate was talking on his cell phone when I walked through the door. He was having an argument with the person on the other end. Somehow my roommate was cheated of whatever amount of money he deserved. Longer this conversation went on the more my roommate got fed up began threatening the life with whomever he was speaking. He popped open a long neck bottle of Budweiser, made a round of phone calls. He wanted nothing to do with me.

Doorbell rang. He stormed up the hallway. Moments later I heard the voice of a Spanish woman speaking broken English. She was pissed. Something about money he owed. He came back at her with the same bullshit. Two of them were walking up and down the apartment one after the other hurling insults. I sat quietly reading the newspaper. I heard her sputtering in Spanish as her voice got closer to me. She reclined on a sofa in the other room. I could see her through the French glass doors. I made my way to the kitchen. She appeared tired in blue jeans and dirty sneakers scratching at needle marks.

I stood holding a glass of water when my roommate walked up and ordered the woman into the bedroom. She didn't quite understand him. He pulled her off the sofa. She kept cussing at him as they made their way towards the bedroom. The door closed behind them. I thought against reading the newspaper. I walked up and down the apartment not knowing whether to stay or go out for a walk. Before I came to a decision I heard my roommate groaning forcing himself into the woman back and forth humping as she screamed.

It seemed exciting at first hearing sounds of two people fucking. Usually in the middle of the night while I was sleeping I was awoken by my roommate and his lovers going at it. He was aggressive and vulgar. His specialty was prostitutes. He treated them like shit, paid them and kicked them out. I never saw most of these women. But often they would come into the apartment. He would fuck them then I would hear the door to the apartment slam shut. I would then go back to sleep.

He had been hanging around "park people." These were people with no where to sleep, drug addicts, young thugs looking for a way out, wretched men and women beaten up by life, many owed money to lone sharks, having to sell their body to pay them back. I had heard my roommate many times in conversation on the phone. I could only imagine who these lone sharks were. But he would beg and plead at the same time stand his ground. Perhaps I was having a nightmare when I thought I heard a man being raped in the apartment by one of these loan sharks.

Oakley was not a loan shark. He was a crackhead. I had a feeling he would be up late reading in a secluded part of the park. When I got onto the grounds of the park I saw a few familiar faces. My roommate had brought some of them over to play chess and cards. I didn't know them by name, basically nodded my head as I made my way through. I found Oakley just as I had thought, sitting by lamplight reading.

"Hey" I said. Bending my head around the cover of the book to see what he was reading. "Oh. *Drama of the Gifted Child*. Alice Miller. I remember that one. Hey. You really shock me you know. I mean the way you go from one genre to the next. Weren't you reading Jack Abbott's *In the Belly of The Beast*? I figured you for a balla. Ever read Jim Thompson's shit? Damn. I swear I might walk in here one night and see you reading Hemingway.

He kept his eyes focused on the book, the light falling over his charcoal black skin. "Wha chu want?" "Ain't seen your ass round here this late before. Them boys might be getting the wrong idea bout you. They be thinking you looking to score some. You wanna get high."

"No," I quickly interrupted. "Ain't bout that. You know me. Y'all come over my place, we sit in a corner, talk, watch the others drink and smoke up. Had a lot on my mind thought I come out here to look for you."

"People see your ass out here they be thinking something different."

"Fuck! Like what?! Yo! Come with me. I buy you a burger. We go sit in a McDonald's or whatever."

We left the park with others indifferent. Perhaps this was something common. He and I walked cool and casual as we made our way out of the park. We got nearer the sidewalks, brighter lights, cars passing, windows from buildings giving off different colors, found our way into a Burger King, ordered, sat down, began eating.

Oakley was older. As he bit into the burger he would talk about the O.G.s who are now in jail. How they stood for something. It gets to a point where you have no education, money or home, drugs become a way of life.

Somehow he was just like me. The difference was I bought an education, seduced girls who went to school in Paris, and sat drinking tea in the morning with my mother for too many years.

DON'T LOOK BACK

BY JANET HAMILL

A Sunday night, late July. I was sitting with friends in a booth at Arturo's sharing two pizzas—onions, peppers and mushrooms, anchovies and olives. I was numb, *sans* appetite. Orpheus, my boyfriend, had been dead for forty-eight hours. I sipped the house Chardonnay, lost in thoughts of bringing him back from the Underworld on Governor's Island.

"Eurydice," my friends said, "Orpheus has no one to blame but himself for what happened Friday night. He was a great poet, no one denies that, but he had this sense of entitlement that made him think he could skip out on restaurant bills. Thank god, he told you to leave the sidewalk table at Da Silvano first, or you both would have been struck by the same truck on Sixth Avenue.

"Now you want to go to Governor's Island and bring him back from the dead. How are you going to do that!? The Underworld isn't on Staten Island anymore. You could easily have gotten a ferry to Staten Island; but they moved the Underworld to Governor's Island last year. No one's going to take you to Governor's Island. The sightseeing ferries that go out there on weekends don't operate at night. Cabbies know that, and you'd have to walk blocks from the subway to the ferry basin. Besides, what would you do if

you managed to get to the basin? Stand around feigning
death in your black slip dress, waiting for the Underworld
ferry to materialize out of the ether?"

Leaving my friends to their pizzas, I stepped onto
Houston Street. I had enough money for a cab, so I hailed
one. I told the driver I wanted to go to the docks at the tip
of lower Manhattan to meet someone. I didn't mention
Governor's Island. When we got there, I said a party boat
would be picking me up in a few minutes.
"You said you were gonna meet someone."
"Yeah, I'm sure he'll be here in a second."
"Lady, I'm not dumb. Party boats don't pick people up
here. They board in mid-town and the South Street
Seaport. "
"Well, this one's making a special stop."
"Sure, whatever. When's this *party boat* bringing you
back?"
"An hour. Two hours."
"Give me a twenty, and I'll be back in an hour."

Fifteen minutes later, a small boat, as if materialized out
of the ether, settled on the water. It was a Venetian water
taxi. On the bow, a figure draped in a long white shroud
stood facing the river. Aside from the water lapping against
the docks, the only sound was of distant music coming from
the boat's cabin.
I called to the ferryman. A tan old man with a shock
of white hair came up on deck, munching on a chorizo
sausage. He looked me over. "What do *you* want?" His
accent was Spanish, which surprised me.
"You're Spanish."
"Carlos Gomez. Cuban."

"I thought you'd be Italian."

"What made you think I'd be Italian?"

"You're operating a Venetian water taxi."

"Ah, the limousine of Venice. Only the best for Hades. He has them custom made."

I told the ferryman I needed to go to the Underworld. Orpheus, my boyfriend, had only been there forty-eight hours. I had to see him.

"You're still breathing. Living souls never make the crossing! I wouldn't mind your company, but I'd catch hell for bringing you."

Carlos turned back towards the cabin. The waves caused by the settling of the ferry calmed. I could make out the music coming from the cabin. "Wait," I shouted. "I know that music."

"You know *that* music?"

"It's Mario Buza and Machito."

"How could *you* know that?"

"I'm from Jersey. I still have relatives in North Bergen. Their neighbors are Cuban."

"No way! You're kidding me! I have relatives in North Bergen. OK, come on. We'll listen together."

In the cabin I danced with my henna head thrown back, the clinging acetate of my slip moving to the rhythms of congas and bongos. Rhumba, rhumba. Cha, cha, cha. Carlos made Cuba Libres. When the record played out, I recited a poem I'd learned from Orpheus, *Dos Patrias* by José Marti. *I have two countries: Cuba and the night . . .*

There were tears in Carlos's eyes when he suddenly said, "I have to take that damned corpse over to the island," he said. "If you stay in the cabin, you can make the crossing, but you're coming back with me, understand?"

Slowly, silently the water taxi crossed the river. The lights of Manhattan receded in behind us and gradually disappeared. There were no landmarks to inform us, nothing to say the water beneath us was the water of the Hudson. In less than ten minutes the island came into view. As the ferry drew closer, a mist rose from the water, green, murky, smelling of sulfur. I could see tall black trees, their tops thick with black leaves. Black birds flew in circles over the tree tops like sentries.

The ferry pulled up to a landing. All was still while Carlos waited for Hades to walk through the gate holding a 'tress passing' sign. "My Lord Hades," Carlos said, bowing.

Hades was a tall, imposing man, long, dark curly hair and a dark curly beard. He was dressed denim overalls and a tee shirt. A pit bull stood at his side.

"I've brought you a new guest."

Two shadows shrouded in burlap stepped out from behind Hades. They lifted the corpse down from the bow and assisted him through the gate.

I couldn't bear it. I ran up on deck. "Hades," I shouted!

"Jesus Christ, what are you doing?"

"I have to speak to him." I jumped off the bow. "Hades!"

"It's her boyfriend. I couldn't stop her. Oh, Jesus Christ!"

I grabbed Hades' overalls. "My name is Eurydice. My boyfriend Orpheus is in there. He's the best poet in New York. He shouldn't be here. It's all a mistake. He was in an accident. He'd still be alive if the staff at Beth Israel knew what they were doing. You have to let me see him. You have to let me bring him home."

"Impossible. Once you've been called as my guest, you're here for eternity. Living souls are forbidden to enter my domain."

"Listen, I'll sing a lyric poem. Anything. What would you like to hear?" I didn't know where the confidence to make the offer came from. I'd learned a few poems from Orpheus. A few. That was it.

"Singing isn't going to change anything."

She's pretty good," Carlos called from the water taxi.

"You stay out of this. You might not have a job after this fiasco."

"Oh, *mi dio*," he said, crossing himself

"Don't blame him. Just tell me what you'd like me to sing."

"I haven't heard music since I became the god of the underworld."

Where the words originated is a mystery, but. I sat on a rock and sang from Sappho, *Standing by my bed/In gold sandals/ Dawn that very/moment awoke me. . . .* and Aristophanes' *The Chorus of the Birds, . . . love is our master alone; like him we can fly/over the ocean and earth, aloft in the sky. . . .* I sang Homeric hymns, Anacreon, I sang for Orpheus, hoping he would hear me. I sang for his life and mine. With all my love, I sang. It was as if Orpheus's gift had been bestowed upon me.

When Hades tapped me on the shoulder, I felt like I was coming out of a trance. He was humming, the black birds singing.

"Eurydice, I've never done this before, but you've brought me such pleasure, I'm willing to make an exception in your case. You can retrieve Orpheus on one condition. Once you find him among the shadows and start leading him out of the cave, you must never turn back to look at him. Until you have both passed through this gate, you must not look back. If you do, you'll lose him forever."

"Lord Hades," I said, dropping down to kiss his sneaker, "How do I thank you."

"Your music thanked me."

Behind the chain-link fence everything was dark and overgrown. I followed a path to the opening of a cave. The descent was steep, the ground wet. Twice I slipped and almost lost my footing. At the base of the cave there was a large lake and arches leading to adjoining caverns. Water dripped from the ceiling and mist rose from the water. Countless shadows stood in clusters. No one spoke.

I cupped my hands and shouted, "Orpheus, Orpheus, it's me, Eurydice." My voice, amplified in echoes, bounced off the cave walls.

Within moments, the shrouded figure of Orpheus came through the arch of a cavern.

"Orpheus," I cried. Perhaps because he'd only been in the Underworld for forty-eight hours, he still maintained his human form under his white shroud. There wasn't a scratch on him. He was carrying his lyre, now fully restored after the accident that crushed them both.

"Eurydice, what are you doing here?"

"I've come to get you. Didn't you hear me singing? I don't know where the words or the melodies came from, but I sang Greek poetry for Hades.

"I did hear you. That was me signing through you. Now you'll always have my gift."

"Orpheus, I want you to keep your gift. You're coming back with me. Hades loved what I sang so much; he's granted me an unprecedented favor. He's letting me bring you back to the living. The same boat that brought you here is waiting to bring us back to the city. When we get there, a cab will be waiting to bring us back to our apartment. We can be home in an hour. Hades has made only one request to insure your release. I can't look back at you. Until we've climbed out of the cave and passed through the gate, I can't look back. If I do, you'll be doomed to this place forever."

With Orpheus following behind me, we started the ascent. We were approaching the opening of the cave when the sound of Orpheus's footsteps ceased. "Are you still there? I can't hear you." Without thinking, I turned around.

"Orpheus! Orpheus!" I stumbled down the steep, narrow path into the cave. There was no response, no sight of him. His lyre lay on floor. I picked it up, making the ascent with it close to my heart.

Later outside the gate, I stood beside Hades and his pit bull.

"When we got to the opening of the cave, I couldn't hear his footsteps. I looked back to see if he was still there."

"I'm sorry. That was your only chance."

"He left this for me," I said, showing him the lyre. "Can I keep it?"

"Of course."

I walked to the ferry. The stern was backed up to the island, the bow facing Manhattan. "I'm ready to go."

Carlos pulled me up onto the ferry.

"I looked back."

"I know. Hades told me."

"Did he fire you?"

"No, I still have a job."

"And I have this," I said, showing him the lyre."

"A lyre and Orpheus's gift of poetry."

It was raining, a warm, steady summer rain, when the cab dropped me off on East 7th Street. I wasn't intoxicated but felt intoxicated by something when I entered the apartment. I turned on the air-conditioner but didn't bother with the lights. The light falling on the bed from the street lamp was as much as my eyes could absorb. The darkness felt comfortable; it made the apartment feel as though it was occupying a liminal zone at the edge of life and death.

I put my head on the pillow, still clutching the lyre. I thought about the new life I'd be starting in the morning. Like Orpheus, I'd spend the day down in the subway at Union Square, signing, reciting, playing the lyre, listening to coins hitting the velvet lining of the lyre case. I picked up Orpheus's worn copy of Rilke and read, *Be ahead of all parting as if it had already happened, like winter as it parts* . . . Lacing the words together for my first poem, a poem about the liminal world and its momentary joys, I fell asleep.

AT THE HUNGARIAN
BY RESA ALBOHER

I was between jobs again, don't ask what I do, it doesn't matter, and I am not proud of my work, and so better not to have to go into it, and so I was sitting in the Hungarian Pastry Shop drinking their bottomless cup of coffee to the bottom and then some in the hopes of drowning out a hangover, don't ask, I am not proud of my drinking and it is boring to go into it, people drink and I am not a 12 step person and so don't even think of suggesting it to me, I am not one for self improvement. There is no self to improve. Don't you read Eastern Philosophy? So what is the point of sitting in circles and sharing our feelings and our desperate humiliations in a florescent lit basement room smelling of mold and stale coffee when the self we are trying to improve is a fiction? The coffee at the Hungarian wasn't stale like in those dreaded basements and everyone in there this early in the morning looked like they had been out all night and had come there directly to this café for the same reason that I had. I was reading a book. A real book, not some fucking reader tablet thing that reduces the world's wisdom to something a lady can stick in her purse. A genuine book with faded yellow pages. A book I had been carrying around with me for a few decades by then. *Zen Comments on the Mumonkan*. Have you read it? An old professor had given it to me. He was my professor so long ago and at the time he was old so he was an old professor in both senses of it. I had studied religions with him in a school outside the city, at a time when leaving the city seemed possible, and a time when religions seemed meaningful and he had said to me once when I was walking across the Quad (ah a quad, so quaint in its dappled green) they can't all be right. What? The sunshine was in my eyes and on that day too I was in extreme hangover mode and thinking of coffee . . . only coffee . . . What isn't right? The world's religion's, they can't all be right. One day you just have to pick one, or go full circle back to the one you were born with. Or give up all together and become an atheist or a tree hugger. He was having a bad day. The university was trying to get rid of him, and he was losing the fight. Come to my office; I am giving away my books. You can't give them all away. They're your books, man. Later that day I went to his office and he gave me this book, this very one, that I was holding in the Hungarian as I nursed my bottomless cup, not quite reading it, not quite not. I had been interested in Buddhism then. He smiled mysteriously. You might as well start with this bastard, that is what he said. I then read the first section on the Koan MU. What the fuck. Does a dog have Buddha nature? Who the fuck cares? I was angry then. I still am. At that time, I used to kick dogs, of course they weren't Buddha's. My anger got the best of me. And no, don't tell me about anger management programs—they are also for the most part held in moldy basements and moldy basements, well, I might as well be dead in one, they feel like a slab in the morgue. As I was pondering MU over my coffee, a woman sat down at the communal table. I tried to scowl to ward her away, but she wasn't having any of it. She was not the type to be warded away by anything.

She looked like she could stand her ground in any situation. She was wearing a red scarf around her shoulders and had dyed red hair and lipstick to match and I could start singing the lady in red to her. I could. And I would. I am just like that. But my voice was too horse to sing, and my throat still burned from the whisky from the night before. So I sat there in silence but in my head I was singing. In another age she would have been the kind of woman to wear a little black hat with a veil. I could see her in it and could see her lighting a cigarette and using a cigarette holder. Ah those days, we'll never get them back. I yearn to smoke in a bar with a woman like this. What I would do to light up right now. Who will ever again know that pleasure, that freedom. And the flirtation that goes with it, may I give you a light my dear? Words of beauty like those haven't been spoken in our city in a long, long while. She was texting on her phone. She would wait for the reply and then text furiously again. Who was she texting? It seemed serious and she was biting her lower lip as she typed into her phone. Her phone was in a sleek rhinestone covered holder. I could cover you in rhinestones my dear if you give me the chance. Diamonds, no. My diamond days are over. But rhinestones, well, even in my recent luckless years, I could muster a rhinestone or two. Her texting made a delicate patter like rain and as she typed the cathedral bells from St. John the Divine started to ring. I once saw the Dalai Lama there, in the days when I believed in something. Before this bland stretch of dismal gloom that was my current life. And before the sour taste of cheap whisky and a bag of salty chips, which had been, my diet for many months now had taken over any other taste in my life. The bells and the typing were hypnotic though, and I felt lulled in a way I hadn't felt in quite a while. When was the last time I was lulled like this? I couldn't remember. But that is a lie, of course I remembered. How could I not. The last time I had felt lulled like this was when I was walking during an insomniatic night in a snowstorm in Riverside Park. The city was disappearing into a blinding mist and hardly anyone was out. Just a few homeless men and me. I had the park nearly to myself. The river was boiling over with white caps as the snow fell, and there was a feeling of sound being swallowed into the snow, and in the heart of the wild weather there this calm, this silence that descended. My work hadn't gone well that day, I had had to do something unpleasant, something I am not proud of, something I will never reveal, but something I would do exactly the same way without any changes at all for such is my character. I have the wisdom to know who I am. That I never have changed, never will change, that in this life of change I am the only constant, my stupid acts something I have come to count on, but in my sleep, I was haunted by what I had done, so I didn't sleep for long and went out into that storm and half hoped to be swept away by it, but instead found this heart of calm I didn't think possible, and I just stood there watching the river disappear into the swirling whiteness. The bells right now gave me a glimmer of that same calm, and as I drank my coffee, I thought for a moment, I could change. I could. I could start a new life. Throw out the old. Atone. For what, I will not say. I am a reticent man. As the woman kept typing more furiously now into her rhinestone phone, pulling her red scarf closer around her as if that would give her some kind of comfort, and as the bells began to fade, I wondered, in her texting conversation was she changing her life as well. What was the person texting with her saying to make her face look so serious, so grim? And what was she saying in response. Your life is unfolding in front of me you amazing creature, it is changing in front of my eyes, you beauty, I can see it in the curl of your lip, and you have no idea. You have no idea my dear that I am now part of your conversation, part of your world, and I am in your life now forever, you can never get rid of me now, my lady in red. Shall I sing it? I bet you would love it my beauty. I can see you in that black netted hat and you are stunning, do you know how stunning you are? I started to feel the hangover lift, and suddenly felt hungry for a real man's breakfast of bacon, eggs, potatoes and toast. Fried heaven. There was a diner around the corner that students go to because it's cheap, much like this café. I was a student once. I asked the big questions. And the old professor, he was right. They can't all be right. They can't. For how would that be possible? There either is a god or there isn't. The Buddha either saw something or he didn't. The barking dog has the Buddha nature or he doesn't and frankly who the fuck cares. There is no place for dogs in any heaven of mine. You can have the sickly beasts. You can take them all and get them out of my site before I start kicking them again. I felt a wave of happiness as the woman continued texting and as I left the café to walk to the diner, there was a promise of snow in the air. I could taste the greasy goodness and the clogs of fat waiting for me. I left the woman texting. She might text into eternity. And then when we meet someplace in that blessed eternity on some street of some city by some river, that has the magnitude of this street, this city this river, with the buildings as majestic as these engulfed in blinding, but gentle, gentle snow, I will forget finally all that I have done, it will all disappear into the snowy mist, and I will reach out to her, this lady in red, dare I start singing, dare I start singing right now as in some distance they are frying up the bacon for my heart attack breakfast, and

I will take her in my arms, pull her close and with such force that I will wipe that serious look off her face forever and she will never have the need to text again. But first I will ask her, in my most debonair voice, mysterious beauty, may I give you a light?

THE MAN WITH TEN HATS
BY L. SHAPLEY BASSEN

On the last day of August, 2004, Marwa al-Hal was arrested during a demonstration outside the GOP Presidential Convention in New York City. She was about to begin her junior year as a Presidential Scholar at Fordham, and she was arrested with another Presidential Scholar, a senior, her boyfriend James-Beekmans. During the slow interrogation, incarceration, and her sudden, surprise release, Marwa responded to her accuser (*Satan* meant 'accuser'—Marwa called him *Officer Iblis*) that she was definitely not an idealist of any kind, "I don't have illusions," she said, "I'm one of those people who sees through to nothing."

Marwa enjoyed her interrogator's ignorance. *Iblis* was Satan's Muslim name; the quotation about illusion was from a Flannery O'Connor short story about a PhD whose wooden leg is stolen by her Bible salesman lover who leaves her helpless in a barn. After her 9/11 injury, Marwa's synesthesia hadn't returned with her eyesight. She saw the world differently and thought, what if her mother's TV psychic were right, that there was no death, death was an illusion, a test, but one you were forced to take blindly. Which was how she felt, blind, once her colors were gone. The legless woman's name had been Joy Hopewell, but she changed her name to Hulga because it sounded ugly. To Marwa, Hulga sounded like a character out of *Iceland's Bell* that she'd read over and over three years before.

Her boyfriend James-Beekmans and most other demonstrators were not released as quickly as Marwa had been; the Company, which moved in time as in space, half perceived, half created her future. Everyone called James-Beekmans by both names as if they were one. He was very tall and very black and mistaken as a basketball player for Fordham University, but not for very long after you met him. James-Beekmans had grown up in a neighborhood near Fordham, Belmont, the Bronx's Little Italy.

"Just west of the Bronx Zoo that I thought belonged to my grandfather because he took me there like *daily* when I was little," James-Beekmans said.

"You were never little," Marwa replied.

He had grown up fighting and defeating white boys who considered him an alien in their territory, when, as he had explained it to Marwa, *his* people had owned and were buried in land in New York City since the 1700s.

"You know the South Street Seaport," James-Beekmans asked on their first date back in January. "That Beekman Street? That's us, we're Beekmans, and we dropped the master's apostrophe 300 years ago. We moved north into Manhattan woods and swamp before Olmsted started terraforming Central Park, and we got run out of *there* when that real estate became worth something, but once we were in the Bronx, we stood our ground. My mom's grandfather took photos of the Italians when *they* first arrived, and he delivered mail to the ones who could read."

James-Beekmans and Marcus got along fine when Marwa introduced her Stuyvesant High classmate to her boyfriend on a hot Sunday at the beginning of August when Marcus was in the City for the weekend, down from "Cambridge."

"Why don't you just say Harvard?" Marwa said.

Marcus had the September *Scientific American* in his hand, and James-Beekmans said, "You ever wonder why the September issue comes out at the beginning of August?"

Marcus looked at the cover, "Special Issue: Beyond Einstein," and answered, "All the time."

Marwa took the magazine out of Marcus's hand and riffled through it to a dog-ear at "The String Theory Landscape" and read aloud, "'According to Albert Einstein's theory of general relativity, gravity arises from the geometry of space and time, which combine to form space-time. Any massive body leaves an imprint on the shape of space-time, governed by an equation Einstein formulated in 1915. The earth's mass, for example, makes time pass slightly more rapidly for an apple near the top of a tree than for a physicist working in its shade.'"

Marwa paused, her eyes having cast ahead, and she read the next words aloud more slowly, as if to herself, "'When the apple falls, it is actually responding to this warping of time.'"

The three undergraduates were standing on the esplanade at Battery Park City looking west over the Hudson. Marwa turned her head around briefly towards the great absence of the Towers. Both young men translated her glance. Marcus quickly drew Marwa's attention back to the article's authors and said he was hoping to do grad work with the one at Berkeley, "on the holographic principle, relating space-time geometry to information content."

Later, Marwa mistakenly thought that James-Beekmans had liked Marcus for always answering a question with another question, but it was because Marcus had in that moment distracted her from falling bodies, her memory of escaping with her younger brother Joey from his elementary school near Stuyvesant High.

Marwa handed him the magazine back and said, "I'm not into science so much anymore since my colors are gone."

Marcus laughed, "Yeah, you're into James-Beekmans."

"This one's going to the *real* Cambridge," she said patting his dark forearm, "all expenses paid on a Gates magic carpet."

Marcus looked impressed at the mention of the new scholarship, Bill Gates's American answer to the primo British Rhodes.

"I'm applying for one," James-Beekmans corrected.

"When's the deadline for that?" Marcus asked.

"You've got to be a senior," Marwa explained.

"Duh," Marcus said.

"November 1st," James-Beekmans answered, "for a Master's."

"In?" Marcus said.

"Anthro."

"*Biological* Anthropology. An anthropological *geneticist* after medical school," Marwa said.

"Are you sure you aren't Jewish?" Marcus teased, "You sound just like my mother."

The threesome had walked in the direction of the ongoing building of a new "Teardrop Park" on the esplanade, and looked down through the fencing at the hardhat workers pouring concrete, at the arranged boulders and another crew of workers planting trees and small shrubs. Leaning against the protective fence for a better look was Joey's friend Ositadimma Bem. The boy recognized Marwa and grinned upward at the height of James-Beekmans. The child gestured basketball dribbling and shooting. James-Beekmans smiled back, shaking his head.

"Hey, Marwa, this park is gonna be so great!" Osita-dimma Bem said.

"Watch out you don't fall in before it even opens," Marwa said.

Marcus picked up several loose stones near Ositadimma's feet. Marcus started juggling them to distract the boy, moving him back away from the fence altogether.

"Can you do more?" Ositadimma asked.

"Try me," Marcus said, angling one palm to receive one, two, three more stones. He was juggling six when one dropped, and he hissed a curse, surprising James-Beeksmans. Ositadimma quickly picked up the stone and tossed it back to Marcus, who was keeping the other five up in the air. This time, Marcus kept all six up and down and sideways for several minutes. Ositadimma whistled admiration.

"How d'you *do* that?"

Marcus caught the stones and tossed the boy one. "You can do that, right?"

Ositadimma tossed it hand to hand easily, impatiently. Marcus put three stones in his shorts pocket and tossed two back and forth, hand to hand, keeping their height level. He threw one to Ositadimma, and the boy imitated.

Marcus called for the two back and juggled three. "You watching?"

"Gimme."

Ositadimma again imitated the pace and arc.

"You want four?" Marcus asked.

"For later," the boy said, concentrating. He stopped juggling and held the stones in one hand, reaching out for the remaining three which Marcus gave him.

"Try using balls of the same size and weight instead of stones," Marcus suggested.

Ositadimma nodded. "There's a lot more to this," he said.

"Just stay clear of the fence," Marcus said. "Don't lean on it."

Ositadimma ignored the warning. Marcus, Marwa, and James-Beekmans watched the neophyte walking away and trying to juggle at the same time.

"He'll have Joey doing that now, y'know," Marwa said. "Something you picked up at Harvard?"

"The masters are at Caltech. It's not really the number you keep in the air, it's the throwing sequences that are interesting. There's only one law, no matter what the tempo, one hand can make only one throw at a time. You can increase the height of one throw in a sequence so long as you equally decrease the height of another throw that lands later, but you have to know how much later, or—"

"Or else," Marwa said.

"Well," Marcus said, "you asked."

Walking back to the reopened Chambers Street subway to return to their various locations uptown and in the Bronx, Marwa talked about Joey and Ositadimma Bem, how his Nigerian name meant 'May things change for the better or be better from today & forever,' "and Bem means peace."

"Sounds like that song from *Norma Rae*," Marcus said.

"Would that you had your ukulele with you," Marwa teased.

In response, Marcus started singing, *"So it goes like it goes/ Like the river flows/ And time it rolls right on/ And maybe what's good gets a little bit better/ And maybe what's bad gets gone. . ."*

"Good thing you're a mathematician," James-Beekmans said.

"Oh, he knows all the Academy Award-winning songs, "Marwa said. "What year was that?"

"1979," Marcus said.

"*To Kill a Mockingbird* was 1962," James-Beekmans said. "That's the only one I know the year of."

"*Days of Wine and Roses* was '62," Marcus said. "I only know the songs."

"He knows them in order from 1934," Marwa said, "please don't get him started."

That night back at the beginning of August, when Marwa and James-Beekmans had returned from meeting Marcus, they went to dinner at his parents' home in the Bronx. Inside the row house it was air-conditioned against the humid heat, but the two were sitting outside on back steps that overlooked a small, neatly planted garden and driveway, part of a common space of garages and gardens behind the attached homes. Marwa's wavy hair was twisted and barretted up on her head. James-Beekmans stroked away some shine of sweat from her long, lovely neck and played with the wetness between his thumb and first finger. His touch evoked an involuntary purring sound from Marwa's larynx. Shocked, she dropped the draft of his Gates personal statement essay that she had been reading. Picking it up, she cleared her throat.

"What's wrong?" James-Beekmans said.

"Nothing. *The Hobbit and Goliath* is a great title," Marwa said. "It's great the way you put them together and then together with *blond* mummies in China with *tattoos*! I didn't know about these early hominid migrations to Indonesia, South Africa, China. I *love* the Cherchen Man," she searched a page. "A tattooed woman with red yarn pierced earrings who was over 6 feet tall, and he was 6'6" with ten hats. *Ten Hats*!" Marwa stopped. "Do you *have* to go to med school to be a geneticist, anthropological or otherwise?"

"You ask my mother that question," James-Beekmans said, "but wait till I'm out of earshot." He imitated his mother's voice, "'Your father and I haven't commuted our asses to 23rd Street to a VA Hospital for three decades for you to——'"

"Spare me her colorful language," Marwa said.

"What did Marcus swear when he was juggling?" James-Beekmans asked.

"'Heat-waste,'" Marwa answered.

"Do any of you Stuy kids ever say anything that's *not* an allusion?"

"Probably not. It's from a sci fi story, "Spell My Name With An S" by Asimov. These energy beings without bodies change a nuclear physicist's career, his whole life, just by changing the first letter of his name from Z to S."

"Heat-waste?"

"I guess to pure energy beings, heat-waste is obscene."

"Spelling our last name without that slave apostrophe *was* a big deal," James-Beekmans said

"My last name is my father's," Marwa said. "I like the way they do it in Norway, I think. A girl gets her mother's name with *dottir* as a suffix, and a boy gets his father's with *son* . . . Oh, it's so *hot!*" Marwa pulled her damp skirt free from where it was sticking to her behind and the backs of her legs.

"Heat outdoors, parents indoors," James-Beekmans said. "Candide's choice?"

"Do *you* ever say anything that's not an allusion?"

"The past dies last in language."

"Who said that?" Marwa brightened.

"I just did. So what should I call you? A nickname? *Ekename* in Old English," James-Beekmans said, "just means 'another name.' Cross-word puzzle; I *had* to look it up."

"So what d'you want to call me?" Marwa said.

"What d'you want to call me?"

Marwa blushed. Then James-Beekmans stood up, took her in his arms, and kissed her.

HEY GERRY!
BY MICHAEL SCHWARTZ

The Cyclone was looming on the horizon. Waiting. I could see it in the distance. I could hear the screams. People were being chewed up and spit back out onto the hard pavement below. All my life I'd heard stories. When I was growing up I knew it was always there, two blocks from my building, waiting for me. I made a vow to God very early on that you couldn't even *drag* me on that prehistoric roaring monster on the verge of collapsing at any moment. When I was thirteen years old they dragged me, with complete disregard for my vow. Thirteen years old. The age, the rabbis told us, when you become a man. I tried to escape, but once you're in the only way out is to get to the other side, unless you want to humiliate yourself by squeezing back through the long line of people behind you to exit through the entrance. I *wanted* to humiliate myself. But they wouldn't let me. The next thing I knew I was in the seat. They lowered the bar. They locked the lock. They pulled the lever. "No. This isn't happening. This isn't real. I'm gonna wake up right when we get to the top and see that it was all just a bad dream." The smell of the old wood withering away in the saltwater air was leaving splinters in my pounding heart as we slowly ascended that first and highest hill, all the other rides below turning into little toys as we clanked closer and closer to the almost 90 degree angle drop waiting for us over the edge. "Help! I'm being kidnapped! I don't think I can survive the feeling of my stomach shooting up to my face oh my God please help me God I'm too young to die how can you let this happen I'm just a thirteen year old boy! Is this really locked? It *better* be locked there's no turning back *now*, I can't believe this is happening!! Why God, *why?!?* I know, I know, I'm a no good, good for nothin' non-believer who quit Hebrew school at nine years old only one and a half weeks after I started but at least I eventually wound up getting a Haftorah tutor once a week and then finally went through with the bar mitzvah, ya gotta give me *that aaaaaaaaaaaaaaaaaaaaaaaaaaaaaaaaaaaahhh-hhhhhhhhhhhhhhhhhhhhhhhhhhhhhhh!!!!!!!!!!!!!!!!!!!* What? Huh? I did it? I did it. I *did* it!" I was down the hill going up the next one, and I was *alive*, I was *still alive!* And I was *laughing!* Louder than anyone else! Even *God!* The feeling of my stomach going up from going down such a steep hill wasn't as bad as I thought. I mean it was bad, but kind of in a good way, like falling from the sky in a dream and as you're about to hit the ground, waking yourself up just in time to save your life, and as my stomach went up going down each successive hill that feeling started to be more and more of a thrill and the laughter got faster and faster with each violent turn *slamming* into each other *harder* and *harder!* And then the ride was over. "What? That's it? . . . I wanna ride again!"

We had gotten on for free because when we were waiting in line Artie Weinberger yelled out: "Hey Gerry! Could we get on one time for free?" Artie learned to do that when his friend Freddie Herring did that and got him on for free and Freddie Herring learned to do that when *his* friend Louie Pinto did that and got *him* on for free and Louie Pinto learned to do that when *his* friend Hector Rivera did that and got *him* on for free and Hector Rivera learned to do that when *his* friend Sammy Sez-so did that and got *him* on for free and Sammy Sez-so didn't learn it from *any*one. He invented it. He was friends with Gerry. Pinto, Rivera, Herring, and Sez-so were thugs from 16th Street, between Neptune and Mermaid, the wrong side of the Stillwell Avenue station tracks. Gerry was Gerry Menditto, operations manager of the Cyclone. We thought he was the Godfather.

I told my friend Frankie from my building about it and we decided it was *our* turn to be Gerry's friends, so the next day, we snuck past the ticket booth, waited in line, and yelled out over the chatter of the other people waiting and the screeching screams of the riders and deafening rattle of the roller coaster cars careening across the ancient rickety wooden tracks right above our heads: "Hey Gerry! Could we get on one time for free? . . . Please?" On the other side of the Cyclone's only stretch of horizontal tracks, Gerry sat there behind his desk next to the big red and yellow lever that set the whole thing in motion every two minutes. With his broad but slightly slouching shoulders, his dapper combed back silver hair and his jutting Brando jaw, he eyed us dubiously like the guardian of the gates to the holy mountain that he was, Saint Peter in a T-shirt up on his folding chair throne, as we poured on the poor innocent ride-deprived local kids with no money look, until he finally gave a very slight head nod toward the first U-turn bend in the tracks that led to the ascension. It worked! We were in! Anointed. Blessed. Frankie and I furtively smirked at each other, then quickly looked away.

As we waited to board, the smell of the old wood didn't taunt me like it used to. This time it tantalized me and I felt a tingling throughout my body. And there it was, the last car, hungry for our bones. Fortunately someone else's bones had already reserved the last car first so we got into the front car. A little less violent but more death defying to the eyes. When the ride was over two minutes later we got up and wobbled back out onto the street. We felt sexy and dangerous. We'd turned a corner in our lives. Anything was possible.

"Hey Gerry! Can we get on one time for free . . . just one ride . . . please?" Every other day: "Gerry!" At first we were amazed each time he gave us the nod, but after a while we began to feel a sense of entitlement. "Of course he's letting us on, it's us, the boys of Luna Park—the Lunatics." We started getting our friends on and one time I even got my older brothers, and my older cousins visiting from Teaneck, New Jersey on. I felt proud . . . powerful . . . A guy who can make things happen . . . A neighborhood mover and shaker . . . The Coney Island Kid . . . Connected . . . Tight with Gerry.

It was time for Frankie and me to expand our operation, branch out a bit. We decided to start going around to the other rides and telling them Gerry from the Cyclone asked if we could please get on one time for free. We knew what an important person he was, so it had to work. And anyway, his nod was becoming more and more subtle, almost imperceptible, which confirmed that he was so crazy about us he didn't even *have* to nod anymore. It was just understood.

For the next week the two of us hit every twisting, whipping, dropping, bopping, thumping, bumping, flying, upside down ride in Coney Island, from the Eldorado disco bumper cars on the south side of Surf Avenue; to the early 1900s antique organ playing B & B Carousel on the north side of Surf Avenue; to the Enterprise and Music Express in Astroland; to the Scrambler, Spookarama, and Wonder Wheel on Jones Walk; to the smoke spitting Dragon's Cave on the Bowery right next to Schweikert's Walk where the Bobsled used to be before the bulldozers came; to the deceptively terrifying Wild Mouse on West 12th Street; to the resplendently decrepit Thunderbolt roller coaster, defiantly still running, the lonely wooden house over which it was built mysteriously still inhabited, big dogs inside the windows barking at the boardwalk to the patient bemusement of its towering next door neighbor the Parachute Jump, which we would have tried to get on too if it wasn't for the fact that the Parachute Jump had been closed down for as long as I could remember.

Our friends didn't recognize us anymore. We walked around with our bodies slightly slanted, our heads slightly tilted, a far away look in our eyes and our faces frozen in a giant, teeth baring, ear to ear grin, just like the exalted funny face of Steeplechase the Funny Place, which had watched over Coney Island for sixty-one years until real estate baron Fred C Trump and his cronies had a brick throwing party one month before my first birthday, smashing it in and tearing it down before we ever had a chance to see it.

One day after we'd gotten on the Water Flume for free we were sticky with summer heat and humidity and needed another cold splash right away as we made our daily rounds. Although we were hesitant about hitting the same ride two days in a row, we figured the Water Flume guy would be too hot and tired to bother to wonder. We said "Gerry from the Cyclone asked if we could please get on one time for free," just as we'd said the day before. But the heat didn't cause him to be a pushover. It caused him to be cranky . . . cost conscious . . . suspicious. "Wait a second," he said in his seething Brooklyn accent. Then he picked up the phone and started dialing. Frankie and I looked at each other nervously. Was he calling the cops? Should we run? The man mumbled something into the phone, listened, mumbled again, then hung up, and with glaring eyes hitting us harder than the rays of the relentless sun, he said, "Gerry wants to see you at the Cyclone right away."

All we had to do was go hide under the boardwalk for a bit, then mix in with the crowd on the beach, cool off with a jump in the ocean, make a quick stop at Philip's old fashioned candy store and scrounge in our pockets for enough change to chip in for one last chocolate egg cream with two straws, and one final chocolate covered frozen banana with crunchies, then go straight home, lay low for awhile, never try to get anymore free rides, and in time the whole thing would blow over. We didn't have to go face Gerry at all. But we thought that as soon as Gerry sees it's us he'd say, "Oh it's you! Why didn't he say so? Okay. I'll call him back to tell him to let you on the Water Flume right away." We couldn't accept the possibility that it could all be over.

We got to the Cyclone, imperiously marched past the ticket booth man, and pushed through to the front of the line as older kids grumbled, "Hey punks, whadaya think you're *doin!?!*"

"Gerry wants to see us," we shot back, "so move aside."

And there he was, sitting at his desk like Vito Corleone in his office during his daughter's wedding. I had an urge to say, "Godfather, may your daughter's first child be a masculine child." But instead we just stood there looking at him until he noticed us. I was hoping he'd just nod as usual.

I'd never heard him speak before. This time he didn't nod. He spoke.

"Who da hell are you?!? I don't even know who you are!!!"

"We're Sammy Sez-so's friends."

"Sammy *Who?!?*"

"S-S-S-Sez-so."

"S-S-S-*Sez*-so?!? ... ... Ohhh, *Sez*-so.

"Yeah."

"WHO DA HELL IS HE?!? I don't know no *Sez-so!!!* How dare you use my name to run a con game, *all over Coney Island?!?* Yooz got a lotta nerve, ya know dat!?! "Who da hell duh yiz THINK YOU *ARE?!?"*

Sweat was pouring uncontrollably down my face burning my eyes but I didn't dare move a muscle to wipe it off as Gerry unleashed his wrath upon us in front of all those innocent people waiting to ride the Cyclone, and Frankie and I prepared to die.

"Get the hell out of here... I don't ever want to see your *FACES AGAIN!!!"*

Everyone stared as we lowered our heads and squeezed our way back through the gauntlet of people we had just cut on line, went back past the ticket booth man without daring to look up at him, and exited through the entrance.

Banished. We'd been banished. Still alive. But banned for life. Frankie and I crossed Surf Avenue back to Luna Park, and walked slowly up West 8th Street, in total silence. When we got back to our building we walked up the staircase to the second floor where Frankie lived, but before he got out to go to his door, we finally glanced in each other's eyes, and for a second, with a sudden fluttering of our lips out of their stunned horizontal straightness, the corners turning back up almost imperceptibly, not into a smirk or a giant grin, but into the tentative beginnings of a simple smile, we shared something secret, something profound; we knew something new but we didn't know what it was, just that it was different. And then we said something, our first words since our banishment:

"See ya."

"Yeah . . . See ya."

WALKING TO CONEY ISLAND
BY PUMA PERL

I don't remember why we decided to walk to Coney Island. I remember that it was November, and JFK was dead, and there were Beatle songs playing everywhere.

Maybe we decided to walk to Coney Island because our parents worked on Saturdays, or because the other girls were prettier, or because we read too many books. Or maybe it was because my socks didn't match, and she slept on a pull-out couch, and we were always picked last for relay races.

I don't remember whose idea it was, but I remember that we marched in step, using our umbrellas as walking sticks. To pass the time, we talked about the Beatles. She loved Paul the best, and I wavered between John and George, always concealing my secret longing for Paul, since he was hers.

We sang *Do You Want to Know a Secret?* as we walked beneath the elevated subway line along McDonald Avenue. She loved that one as much as I did, despite the fact that it was sung by George. McDonald Avenue was always dark and depressing, and the stretch between Quentin Road and Kings Highway contained several chicken slaughterhouses; we pulled our scarves over our faces to ward off the bloody death smells and trudged on.

The day turned damp and bitter. She wore a blue plaid skirt and a short jacket, and her legs were bare. I had on my usual baggy jeans, sneakers, and green parka. There was a dungaree factory near my building, so all of my pants were bought there at a discount, regardless of how ill fitting and unflattering they turned out to be. She never complained about the cold, although I could see that she was shivering; I envied her smooth legs and short white go-go boots.

The streets were nearly deserted. At one point, a tough-looking boy rode by on a rusty bicycle, a transistor radio blaring from his handlebars, and a large box of Fruit Loops in the cart. We laughed but not too loud—the last time we'd made fun of a boy like that, he'd jumped off his bike and hit me with a chain.

Finally, we were able to see the parachute jump, and knew that we were close. We lifted our umbrellas triumphantly as we charged over an imaginary finish line, but our excitement passed as soon as we reached Stillwell Avenue. Broken bottles littered the streets, the rides were closed, and nothing smelled of cotton candy. We stood in front of a boarded up hotel wondering what to do. We were hungry, but even Nathan's looked deserted and uninviting. Coney Island ignored us, like a potential lover who had changed his mind.

Despite the wind, we wandered up to the Boardwalk and back down along West 12th Street. Three guys in black leather jackets lounged against the fence outside the Cyclone, smoking cigarettes and goofing around. As soon as they spotted us, they stopped the horseplay and stood perfectly still, staring at us. The tallest one waved us over while the other two wolf whistled. I knew they were paying attention to us out of boredom, not because they thought we were cute. They were the kind of guys my parents called "hoods," the type that made fun of us if they noticed us at all. I started to cross the street, expecting her to follow, but she grabbed my arm. *Let's go talk to them*, she said, and without waiting for an answer, made her way up the block.

I didn't know what else to do, so I followed. I heard my mother's voice telling me if all my friends jumped off the Brooklyn Bridge, that I would, too. I had never agreed because I was afraid of heights, but I suddenly grasped the meaning of the statement.

Hi! she chirped when she reached them, in a perky voice that I had never heard her use before. *Well, hi ho!* responded the shortest one, imitating her tone. The tall guy shot him a look and he shut up, glowering at us as if it were our fault.

What are you girls doing out here? Besides looking for me, the tall guy asked. His friends guffawed like it was the wittiest thing they had ever heard. Maybe it was. They looked to be about eighteen, old enough to be used to getting into trouble all the time. I was terrified and tongue-tied; this was my usual state of being around any boys, but this time I sensed that we might be in actual danger. She was either oblivious or didn't care.

We were taking a long walk, she said, and reached for his cigarette. I was shocked by her boldness and even more shocked that she knew how to smoke; she didn't choke and she exhaled through both her nose and her mouth.

You want one, too? He asked, not really looking at me. I shook my head.

Oh, she never wants to do anything, she said, and astounded me again by making a perfect smoke ring. All three guys stared at her lips.

She'd turned on me before, usually when she saw a chance to enter a more popular clique. It never really worked out, and I was always there waiting. She was the only best friend I'd ever had, and we were too young to know that our self-loathing was our strongest bond.

These guys may have been high school dropouts, but they were clever enough to read the situation clearly. She was out for trouble and I was in the way. I hunched my shoulders and stared at the ground, regretting that I'd ever left the house. Loneliness and boredom beat the damp cold streets of Coney Island and my rapidly increasing fear.

What's your name? asked the tall guy.

Judy, she responded, *what's yours?*

Judy, he repeated. *What about your little friend? She got a name?*

I felt them looking at me and hated the redness that I knew was rising in my cheeks. I kept staring at the ground.

How old are you? Judy. He pronounced her name in a taunting, sing-song way but she acted as if she didn't notice.

Fifteen, she lied. He smirked at her answer, but didn't challenge her. It probably wouldn't have made any difference if he knew we were only twelve.

How old's the other one, he asked, *twenty-two?*

The reference to me seemed to trigger the shorter guys into action. Suddenly, they were on either side of me. One of them poked me in the chest, and I jumped.

It's alive! he yelled, and they all laughed, even Judy. Actually, I think she laughed the loudest. The other guy pulled my hat off of my head, looked me over and pretended to gag, then shoved it back down over my face.

You look better that way, he said in a nasty tone.

I fixed my hat and saw that the tall guy, who had never told Judy his name, now had his arms around her and was pushing her against the fence. She giggled nervously, but didn't push him away. I was relieved that the other guys immediately lost interest in me, but concerned for Judy.

Come on, Judy Cootie, let's take a walk. I like you. You're cute. Cute little Judy Patootie.

I couldn't hear her response, but it appeared to anger him.

I like you, he repeated, *I wanna make out with you. Something wrong with that picture?*

He pushed her against the fence, grinding up against her. She must have bitten his lip because he jumped back, stared down at her, and slapped her across the face.

Listen Cunt, you came wiggling your fat ass over to me. I didn't send for you. What the fuck you doing down here anyway with your retard friend?

I stood rooted to the spot as the three of them surrounded her, pushing her back against the fence. I was too stunned to run for help and couldn't even open my mouth to scream. It was over as quickly as it had started, and the three of them ran down the block, shoving me aside as they passed.

Bye, Judy Cootie! one of them yelled. *Thanks for nothing, you ugly twat.*

Her jacket had been pulled open and a couple of buttons on her Indian Madras shirt were loosened, showing the top of her white Playtex bra.

Well, you're a big help, she said.

What was I supposed to do? There were three of them. And I didn't even want to go near them in the first place.

They're right—you are a retard, she yelled.

They're right about you, too—you're an ugly twat!

We stared at each other in shock. I had never said anything really mean to her before, much less used a word like "twat."

You're the ugly one, you stupid cunt, she retorted, and stormed down the block. I trailed behind her because I had no idea where the subway was or which train to take. She was the one who always knew things like that.

We sat across from each other on the ride home but didn't speak. When we got off the train, a couple of girls in our class were standing in front of the corner candy store. She started talking with them, as if nothing had happened. I glanced back as I walked away, just in time to see her point at me as they all laughed. I didn't know then that for the rest of the school year I would be branded as the "who-er" that let a bunch of Coney Island boys feel her up in front of the Cyclone.

As soon as I got home, I took a bath. I lay back in the warm water and thought about how mean Coney Island was in the winter. I closed my eyes and pictured beach umbrellas and striped chairs and bumper cars, and wondered how long it would take to walk there in the spring.

FIRE, PAPER, ROCK
BY JACKIE SHEELER

Weekend picnic-table politics commence before the hairy crack of dawn. A vanguard of (always) young and (usually) muscled and (perhaps) hung-over men snap oilcloth over splintered planks and sink sunbrella poles to mark the turf they claim. She watches, smoking, from a bench on Morningside Avenue, not exactly hoping for a fight. Tables are dragged, aligned, upended; moved and moved again. Maps and grandmothers are consulted, borders disputed, compromises occasionally reached. Come scouting for a spot once the sun's up and you're SOL: too late, son. Whyn't you take your people to the beach?

Once their territories are secured, the boys put on headphones and settle in for a long wait. Families, all loud toddlers and bloated shopping wagons (wings, sauces, chips, ribs and carefully-camouflaged flats of beer) trundle over the goose-shit tundra starting around noon.

Living so close to the park, she loathes the miasma of picnic: accelerant and smoldering coal dense as dollar-store cologne before even a single wing or burger sets to sizzling on the grills. She doesn't smoke at this bench on barbecue-permit days. Not with half a dozen hyper-extended families fussing over radios, hibachis and frisbees barely three yards away, just a low iron rail and the back of her bench between them. She didn't want, and didn't want to seem as if she did want, a seat at any of those temporary feasts. Spend all afternoon swatting flies off the Saran Wrap under a hot sun and the cold, watchful eyes of half-a-dozen withered Christian matriarchs? No, she'd rather play Spider on her phone or go dicking around on Facebook. Take a nap. Watch a rerun.

Or—actually, honestly—she'd rather be burning her journals. If she could just bring them here when it was time, when the back-closet milk-crate couldn't hold another notebook, another ribbon, another photo or tiny plastic ziplock full of hair. Bring them here, late at night, armed with a candle, alone.

But no. Too many dog walkers, cops, homeboys, thieves and gentrifiers for such a private undertaking. She'd learned the hard way—that fat Russian bitch in Jackson Heights, lumbering up to the barrel (wasn't it enough, reduced to burning ten years' worth of journals in a sanitation bin? Did there have to be a fat Russian too?). "You cand burn yuhr gahbage here leddy!" For 40 minutes, lumbering through Tai Chi lessons with a graceful flock of elderly Chinese ladies, a dumptruck stuck on Ballerina Island, the chapped red woman watched her drop notebook after spiral-bound notebook into the fire. Only after her crate was empty and the last journal half gone to ash did the woman rumble over. "You cand burn yuhr gahbage here leddy!"

"Are you a moron?" She put her arm up, up and back, took two steps toward the woman. "Are you fucking BLIND that you think a fucking NOTEBOOK is fucking GARBAGE?" The dumptruck shut its mouth and backed away. Backed, not turned. There was fist in the air.

Not doing that again, no. And god forbid the cops. Handcuffs jingling behind her while they log a smoking box of half-burnt books as evidence. Random words, lines, paragraphs still horrifically legible in fat blue Flair under their pale grey glaze of char. She'd rather die.

Old journals cannot be shredded: any paper fed through a shredder is instantly degraded to the level of memorandum or makework. Therefore, as long as there is handwriting there will, sooner or later, be books to burn. But don't, as they say, try this at home. Not here, in the capital of smoke-alarms and busybody neighbors.

Go to enough 12-Step meetings in Manhattan and sooner or later you'll hear a story (likely followed by a joke) about somebody trying to burn their Fourth Step, tradition-ally done after completing Step Five. Whole kitchens have been set ablaze, bathtubs destroyed, dogs and cats terror-ized, spouses confused, apartments lost. It's almost a recovery rite of passage, this further fucking up of your life while trying to burn the written account of just how much you fucked it up before. And Fourth Steps are just a couple pages; she's looking at hundreds (thousands?) of potentially incriminating leaves.

So these odorous weekend barbecuers with their fat blue-and-white sacks of charcoal, are infuriating reminders of the milk crate overflowing in its closet. She'd never get a permit herself, not in competition with the kind of people who stake out tables before 5 a.m. They probably sleep overnight on the sidewalk outside whatever city agency sells the few sum-mer licenses available. And what if she did get one? Play deaf-and-blind to the Morningside picnickers, torching note-books in a hibachi that she'd thereby deprived some big (hungry) family from using? Way to piss off half of Harlem.

There is one place, superlatively private and supremely inconvenient, that she has used, undisturbed (though not entirely undetected), twice. She found it three years ago, during the Summer of Long Walks. One afternoon, the promenade crowded with joggers and baby carriages, the spot struck her imagination and stuck in her mind: a place to sit, a place for the fire, a wall against river wind and curious eyes. A spot so perfect it could have come with a trumpeting herald of angels. She knew better than to swing over the railing and investigate further during prime-time; she just stopped for a smoke, took some camera pix of the Jersey profile across the river: a photographic map to mark one special patch on the long, unrolling path.

She went back early on a Sunday, before the table stake-out games began in Morningside, before runners, bikes and power-walkers swarmed the Greenway. Swinging a leg over the low fence, she checked for bystanders (none), heaved up the crate, sat on the outside ledge then pushed her ass off the seawall and down onto the rocks, crab-walking slant-wise to the spot. Moss and seaweed glimmered at the water-line; it smelled like a cross between Coney Island and Caesar's Bay. She didn't see the rats, or hear them over the arrhythmic slap of the leisurely river. One stranded fish, shorter than her pinky, gasped in a shallow tide-pool.

By chance she did the hard one first, a plush faux-leather perfect-bound journal with heavy, unlined pages covered front and back with handwriting and glued-down artifacts (photos, a disposable funeral-home veil) from the eighties. Squirting lighter fluid, she tossed match after match onto its etched cover, expecting it to go up all at once, like a Molotov. But the vinyl wouldn't catch, the crumbling pages too dense to pull the air they needed to ignite. She ripped it apart, tore every old page into pieces small enough to fit the little tin knick-knack box she'd brought along almost as an afterthought. Once she figured out what any girlscout would've already known, burning the spirals was cake.

She was no girlscout. But one hell of an improviser. A girl who learns from her mistakes. This is how she'll do it next time, after barbecue season but before it's cold enough to snow.

On the eve: Pack the crate tight, fill the smallest backpack with supplies, put the backpack on top of the crate, drag it all to sit by the door.

On the day: get up before daylight, strap on the pack, pick up the crate—no shower, no coffee—and leave, walking southwest. No public transportation: the overflowing crate is a dead puppy, a torn-off bloody dripping naked leg, a wasp's nest, an orgasm in progress. Keep it carefully away from the eyes of strangers, the riders of buses, the subway sleepers. Walk southwest, make Riverside by dawn, drag the crate down the steps of the carefully-landscaped park terraces, through the tunnel, onto the Greenway. Heave it over the seawall. It must not be dropped.

Now she's a sneak, a fence-climber, an eater of words, a carrier of amputated limbs, an arsonist, an alchemist, a writer. She's two feet above the Hudson River's lowest tide, transmuting language into smoke, and she's taking her own sweet time.

NAKED WOMAN KILLED BY COPS
BY PETER MARRA

1. Memory

"Are you ready?" she said. She was smiling.

"No wait!"

She put the gun in her mouth and pulled the trigger. The night was crimson. Bone, crunch, and soft flesh sounds. The darkness smelled of plasma and heat.

Times Square, 42nd Street, The Deuce. It's all gone now. Scrubbed clean. An essay in boredom. Trite. Gone are the hookers, pimps, runaways, addicts, rivers of cum. No more World 49th where *Deep Throat* premiered. Gone are the *Metropole Go-Go Bar*, the *Pussycat*. Adios *Avon 7,* where one could watch Annie Sprinkle get fisted on stage for a seven-dollar admission while *Houses of the Holy* blared on a never-ending loop; this is the place where you could see Jamie Gillis recite Shakespeare in the nude.

Instead of tourists running away in a gelatinous mass fearful of crime and violence and their daughters being abducted, sold into slavery (or worse), they now straggle down the Deuce staring up at the office buildings, *Madame Tussauds* and admire the bland refurbished theatres that were once fleapits and grindhouses (where you could fuck a man, woman or someone in transition for free). The skeletal decaying remains of *Show World* haunt the west side: a homage to decadent dreams of humans in ecstasy with eyes rolling backwards. At one time you could watch people fucking or a skanky succubus exposing herself in a glass booth for the drop of a token.

Luckily there are still some pockets of perversion here and there in the city. Some exist near Times Square. Some are decaying in Coney Island. Some fester in Jackson Heights. Boiling desire in Staten Island. The beast lives.

2. As Usual

*We are born into here screaming and we leave here
screaming. Some leave quite vocally, some in a more
subdued fashion, but there is always the scream:
external or internal—it's all the same.*

The drummers on the 14th Street station platform were driving her crazy. They were beating empty plastic pails that were once used to hold vinyl compound. Tribal sounds were ripping through the station, deadening the sounds of the subway trains. Maxine looked around at the other "customers" (as the MTA likes to call them) to see if she was the only one bothered by the noise. Other people seemed to be grimacing, and she wondered why they didn't get organized and kill the drummers. They could jump them easily and throw them onto the tracks, right in front of the approaching R train. She ground her teeth in silence. The deep hole in her stomach got bigger. It had started out as a small pinhole this morning but as the events of the day unfolded it grew and grew, eventually morphing into the huge cavern that she felt at the moment.

It was 6:30 p.m. and she was on her way home. The platform was crowded as usual. The drummers were playing as usual. At the other end of the platform, the old Russian man was paying his accordion as usual . . . as usual . . .

Seven minutes came and went and the train still hadn't arrived. The platform was getting crowded with customers and the drummers were taking a rest, although the accordion music was still playing. The announcements were still playing: train arrivals for the opposite direction, opposite from where she wanted to go. Eventually the accordion music stopped, the old man was taking a break, the drummers were taking a break, and the crowd was still humming. Maxine wished she hadn't thrown out the *New York Times*. There was a growing red stain on the platform, smelled like afterbirth. Her stomach twitched slightly. She desired the technicolor to be removed. She craved to be black and white walking in chiaroscuro. Maxine noticed a vendor selling small lacquer boxes, arranged neatly on a card table. So smooth, so pretty. Is she bought one, she wondered, what would she keep in it?

3. Investigation/Memento Mori

No such thing as a peaceful death.
Welcome to the plague years.
The fun times are about to begin.

First Avenue and East 2nd Street. A tenement apartment. The EMT I had called had just left with the corpse. There was a puddle of urine on the mattress. I really hate this. She lit a cigarette and blew the smoke in my face. My eyes teared slightly and I tried to act blasé. She stared at me briefly, then flipped the mane of red hair over her shoulder and laughed. What a bad dye job.

I had to get this information so I was willing to put up with her bullshit and image stroking. She sat down and crossed her black nylon clad legs, simultaneously adjusting her black slip. Seamed stockings, Cuban heels, feet clad in black patent leather open toed high-heels. Aura of Bettie Page.

"So what exactly happened?" I asked.

"Well we had sex; he died. That is that."

"He died while having sex or after sex . . . ?"

"We fucked; he seemed to have a good time. His penis was kinda tiny—I didn't feel very much. I got up to pee. When I came back his face went from purple-to-red-to-blue and he had a surprised look on his face, as if something happened that he didn't expect. Then he arched his back on the bed and then—nothing else. I thought it was sorta funny. I laughed a little—dumb fuck. Then I called you."

"So you actually weren't in the room when he kicked it."

"No I was peeing."

She excused herself and went into the next room, returning with an insulin hypo filled with clear fluid and a leather shoelace. She sat down on a busted leather chair. Staring at me with a defiant look, she extended her left arm and tied off. She slapped her bulging vein a few times, then gently inserted the needle. She smiled as the red blossom entered the needle. The plunger went back and forth a few times.

She released the shoelace and let her head fall back, eyelids lowered and she went pale.

"You have to leave," she said, "It's hard to speak."

"OK. Thanks. I'm going. Bye-bye."

"Bye . . . Bye . . . *Asshole*."

We used to date a few years ago. I felt a pang of loss, but I wasn't sure if I missed her or the drugs.

I left her apartment and walked down the stairs. I snorted, trying to flush the urine smell out of my nose and brain. I felt dirty again. When I hit the street I realized that I had a headache. Brain throb . . . Silence forever and

I was dripping in cold sweat. I had to sit down. I walked down First Avenue to a diner. I entered and sat down. It was empty except for a bored waitress who seemed to resent that I had come in. She had short black hair, a skin tight uniform, and a scorpion tattoo on her left forearm. She moseyed on over and tossed a menu in front of me then stood looking at me.

"Just give me a cup of coffee."

"You can't sit at the table for a cup of coffee. You have to sit at the counter."

"I'm not taking up a fucking valuable table, am I? There's no one here. If someone comes in and really wants this table I'll move to the counter. OK?"

I gave her a couple of bucks so she would leave me alone. She stared at me for a second, took my money and came back with the coffee.

"Actually I don't care where you sit. My boss says I have to state our seating policy."

"OK. Whatever."

She put the coffee in front of me.

"Thanks."

I took a sip of the coffee. It was actually quite good.

My coffee drinking and self-repair was interrupted by the door opening and a very sad female walking in. This woman was cursed. I just knew it. Her black pupils were dilated sucking in everything they saw. A vacuum of fear grabbed me. I shivered slightly and shook my head slightly.

The waitress dragged her ass on over once again with another menu in her hand. The woman walked past her and went to sit at the counter. She sat on a stool and pulled her leather jacket tightly around her shoulders. She ordered coffee also and smiled slightly when she took a sip.

She sat at the counter drinking, every once in awhile briefly glancing over her shoulder to take a peek at me. I debated whether I could go over and speak to her. I made sure my 45 was well hidden. I buttoned my jacket and started to get up from my chair. I was surprised when she got up from the stool and walked towards me. She was somewhat thin and pale, about 5'5", clad in a worn white blouse, worn tight Levi's that showed off her slightly curvy figure; these were tucked into a pair of worn black stiletto boots. The eyes I had previously described burned holes into me; I could actually feel some pain in my chest. I continued to stand up as a courtesy to her as she approached.

The waitress was watching us from her perch in the corner, her eyes narrowing to stare at us every so often, then returning to her copy of *People*.

4. FEAR / *Final Report*

The stink of the subway, the specters boarding; some in shock, some too stupid to realize what is going on.

The scantily clad women leave in silence. Some breathe heavily, heaving. In heat. Somnambulism.

"Maxine," she said in a somewhat raspy voice. She coughed slightly.

"Excuse me?"

"Maxine—that's my name."

"Lovely name."

She sat down and looked me over. I could see that she was trembling slightly as if she were cold, although it was quite warm in the diner and it was a warm October night. The First Avenue traffic had died down to almost nonexistent, which I regarded as rather strange. It was a Tuesday evening around 8 p.m. It should have been blaring noise outside, honking, music, cursing, the street life mutations being heard. It was rather unnerving.

"I write and walk in rage," she continued. "I heard about a woman in Tampa. She was walking down a road nude while carrying an antique revolver in her left hand and a silver dagger in the her right hand. When she came upon two cops on their lunch break, they didn't hesitate to blow her brains out. No warning, no Miranda. There is a news blackout."

Maxine reached into her pocket and pulled out a black lacquer box about one-by-one inch square. Placing it gently on the table, she opened the lid and slightly caressed and rubbed the thing inside which I couldn't see. She carefully placed the cover back on, picked up the box and put it back in her pocket.

"Please bless me," she begged.

Without waiting for my answer. She got up slowly, somewhat shakily and slowly walked to the ladies' room. I didn't know what to do, really. I reached inside my jacket and made sure that my gun had the safety off. She entered the bathroom and locked the door behind her. After five minutes the door opened and she emerged naked, bleeding from her hands and her feet. The blood accentuated her parchment-like skin; translucent and quite gorgeous. She seemed to float towards me. I felt a metallic taste in my mouth and my teeth started tingling. She was only a few feet away from me. I heard her whispering.

"I have a stigmata. My child detests me. Please touch me, then shoot me."

She was getting closer. My memories came flooding back—a torrent of desire. I was alone. For the first time I realized how afraid I had always been.

Maxine collapsed on the floor. The waitress screamed and screamed and will always be screaming. The walls grew warm and we were kissed by shadows, strings of sounds and sweet saliva and sweat encircled us.

There was a growing red stain on the floor, smelled like afterbirth.

OTHER DAYS
BY MARIA KRANIDIS

Lisa always felt lost passing through the unnatural curves of the higher numbered streets, but she somehow always found her way, crossing first with her eyes before her body. She could smell familiar foods and hear music from the windows of first floor apartments. The bakery Mr. Pete told her to show up at for the interview was at the corner of 190th Street and St. Nicholas Avenue.

She saw a line of people outside the shop before she could look in and see the harried man behind the counter. She squeezed through the crowd and called, "Mr. Pete! It's me, Lisa. For the interview."

Mr. Pete looked her up and down while giving change to a customer and yelled, "Go in the back and put on the jacket that's hanging on the wall and come behind the counter and help!"

She quickly did what he told her to do. She left her pocketbook on a shelf dusted with flour and put the jacket on. She felt in the pockets and found bread-crumbs and lint. The back of the bakery was open and cold and huge: two big counters stood in the middle of the room in front of a cold oven. The air was old and sour like yeast. She could see remnants of sesame and flour everywhere.

"I need your help!" Mr. Pete begged. "Stand behind that slicing machine and slice the bread."

She suddenly felt nervous. She had sliced bread using a machine like this before, but that was long ago. She'd forgotten how. Still, before she knew it, the crowd had faded and Mr. Pete was counting out the register. He looked up from his glasses and asked her to wipe down the front of the display cases.

Later, he told her, "You're hired." He unhooked a key from his chain and put it in her hand. "Be here at seven tomorrow morning and put the cakes back in the window display the way you see them now. You think you will remember where they were?" he asked.

"Yes. I will remember," she answered taking off the jacket. She walked into the back to hang it on the wall and could smell the faint scent of perfume.

"May I take this home and wash it?" she asked.

"Do whatever you want," he answered sweeping.

"Good night then," she told him and left.

On her walk to the train station she realized she never asked Mr. Pete about her hours or pay. She didn't think he even knew her name.

On the train home she thought of how the bread felt in her hands and this thought made her hungry. She should've asked her boss for a loaf from the leftover bin.

———

The bodega next door to the bakery was already busy. People were coming out holding coffee. Lisa put the key in the door and turned. The smell was just as sweet and sour as it was the day before. She put her now-clean jacket on, still damp around the pockets. She would try not to lean on anything until it dried. After putting the cakes out in the display window she stood back to double-check and was still not sure she had arranged them as they were the day before.

Suddenly, she realized there was no bread for her to sell. She kept looking at the street waiting for Mr. Pete to show up with the bread. Then she remembered the ad: 50 hours a week, blah, blah, Balkan bakery—no experience necessary. She couldn't remember the phone number. She had to talk to Mr. Pete now. She was alone and didn't know what do. The phone rang. She answered.

"Good—you're there!" said Mr. Pete. "The bread delivery guy will be there shortly. Put everything on display—you know what to do," and then his voice got louder. "Oh, and the register opens with fifty dollars. When you have time, practice writing *Happy Birthday* on wax paper—all the colors are on the back shelf. At night put all the money in a bag with the date and amount on it and put it in the empty flour bin in the back. See you tomorrow." He hung up. He still didn't know her name.

Before long, the delivery van pulled in front of the store and a long tray of hot loaves were carried in by a young man in an all-white uniform.

"Hey, I'm John" he said. "From the Midtown store. We're really busy down there." Then looking around, he put his hands on his hips and shook his head. "I don't know about this place," he said. "Mr. Pete should just shut it down. It's cold," he shivered. "Doesn't feel like a bakery." On his way out he looked back and yelled, "I might be back later with fresh pastries." He drove off lighting a cigarette.

Now, the store was filled with the warm scent of fresh bread as if someone had baked the loaves there. She felt her heart get warm and cozy, organizing the bread on the shelves.

No one came in. Hours passed.

———

After a while, she decided to practice writing *Happy Birthday* on wax paper. The liquid gel came out soft and easy to her touch. But her handwriting was terrible. She wrote out the words 40 times and got better.

What day was it? June 10th? Yes. Lisa realized she had missed mother's birthday. People don't remember the birthdays of the dead. The death date takes its place. Mother would have liked the scarf she spotted in the boutique window on her way home yesterday. She could see her mother smile, tightening it around her neck then pushing her dark hair back with both her hands, putting on more red lipstick, smacking her lips together as if tasting life itself.

"Life is good in New York. I have travelled the seas to be here!" Mother would laugh. But there were other days of headaches from the long hours of cleaning homes and offices all week. She would buy groceries on her way home, put them on the kitchen table and go lie on the couch and mumble, "Cook something please. I'm done." Lisa would find her asleep by the time she was finished making dinner. Many nights she never even woke up to eat, so Lisa would take off her shoes and lift her feet onto the couch. Many times she would find her there in the morning. And now she'd forgotten her birthday.

———

A bald man walked in and asked quickly, "Any pastries?"

"We only have cookies now," she answered. "But we'll have pastries later."

The bald man walked out just as quickly.

Suddenly, she felt anxious. Where was the delivery van? She longed for a store full of happy people, but instead there were empty counters and she became consumed with the same sadness she felt when confronted by abandoned buildings.

Finally, John the delivery guy came back, carrying a long tray of assorted pastries. "Elephant Ears, or Butterflies, whatever you want to call them," he said pointing. "These here are Cheese Danishes and these are Linzer Tarts. Enough to hold you over," he half-smiled. "I'll be making some Black and White cookies later. If I have time, I'll bring you some."

"How's Mr. Pete?" she asked.

"Busy. Very busy," he answered. "Why? Do you need anything?"

"No," she said. John left the shop with a wave.

———

In the weeks that followed, Lisa got to know a few regular customers. The train station was around the corner and the store was usually busy between four and six when people came home from work. One day, she decided to eat a Danish she'd been eyeing all day. It looked sweet and she was hungry. She took a big bite and could taste the vanilla and honey that had been melted in the dough. But as soon as her mouth was full, a customer walked in.

It was the small lady who bought bread every evening on her way home. She looked at Lisa cautiously, put her chin down and declared, "I have lost 120 pounds this past year. I don't eat any bread or sweets. The bread I buy is for my family."

Lisa swallowed the Danish as fast as she could.

"Sweets are not good for you," the lady announced. She paid for her daily bread and left the store.

"Thank you," Lisa whispered, and sat down to finish the Danish.

Again the silence in the store filled her. She remembered her mother smiling a sad, almost childish smile. "I know sweets are bad for me," she would say, "but I love them!" Then she would grab her pocketbook and look at Lisa. "Come on, let's go get some carrot cake and coffee." Lisa now smiled thinking of her mother. Then an unwanted memory came to her. "Give me the shot in my belly today" he mother whined. "My arm is bruised."

When Lisa looked up she saw a young couple standing across the counter.

"Do you have any birthday cakes?" the young man asked.

"Yes," Lisa answered. "Right behind you in the fridge." She walked over to help them.

"We'll take this one." They both pointed to the one with the most flowers on it.

Lisa gently picked the cake up and brought it behind the counter. "Do you want anything written on it?" she asked.

"Happy Birthday, Mom" they both said.

"She will like that," the girl said.

Writing on the cake was easy for her now. Every word fit perfectly. Lisa felt proud of herself. She took the money from the couple and they walked out happily with the cake.

The phone rang—it was Mr. Pete.

"Hey, listen" he said. "Sunday coming up will be the last day for this store. I'm closing it down. There is no profit, so pay yourself and . . . " before he could finish his sentence, Lisa stopped him.

"Really?" she asked him. "What if we had more things to sell, more fresh pastries and cookies? I never have anything to sell!" Her voice was squeaky and she thought she might cry.

"You can always come and work here in Midtown. This store is always busy" he said.

"I guess I should" Lisa agreed. "When should I be there?"

"Monday morning—eight o'clock," he said and hung up.

She felt angry and sad. How could he let this store go? How could he? He had visited the place only three times since she was there, but she had spent every day, all day . . . How could he let it go?

The couple with the birthday cake came back. They dropped the box on the counter.

"This cake is sour!" the young man complained.

"It's terrible," the young woman added. "And it was for my mom's birthday!"

"I truly apologize," Lisa said, her voice barely coming out. She walked to the register, took out money and put it in the young man's hand.

"I'm so sorry," she whispered as the couple walked out of the store.

Lisa sat down on the chair next to the window. Perhaps I should have been standing, she thought. Maybe people passing thought the store was closed because they couldn't see me.

She kept looking at the cake on the counter.

A couple of pieces were missing. She dipped her finger in the frosting, and tasted it. Indeed. It was sour.

CHAMPAGNE AND COCAINE
BY RICHARD VETERE

The game was five card stud. I had been dealt a pair of aces as hole cards, the ace of spades and the ace of clubs. My one up card was the five of spades.

I looked around the table. The ante was two hundred and I had my last remaining five grand in front of me in chips. I was already down a grand thanks to being constantly dealt the second best hand.

There's a saying in poker that if you look around the table and you can't find the sucker it's probably you. I spent the last seven hours looking around the room and I was sure it wasn't me. Mikey Delarosa was down two grand and he played aggressive and stupid. Jimmy 'Chaps' was already down the same and was playing wild and reckless. The black guy from Jamaica, Hilly, was down a grand with just bad cards and Sully, all three hundred pounds of him, was down a few hundred playing everything close to the vest. Only Charlie, Charlie Durrico was the winner, the big winner. So I say, look around the table, if you're not the winner, your luck can only change.

Everyone checked so I raised. I bet two hundred and watched to see who stayed in. Only Sully called leaving Durrico to bet. He looked at me and smiled. "Raise," two hundred more.

He had a king of spades in front of him so I took him for a pair of kings. Sully went out and I called. I thought I could raise again but I stopped myself.

Jimmy was dealing and my next card was the nine of spades. Durrico got a six of spades. I was still ahead in my thinking so I bet four hundred. Durrico paused and called.

I had to figure him for kings now. I figured he called because that's the way winners sometimes are. They are on a streak so they call everything figuring they're going to hit it. He must have figured he'd pull a third king or another pair. He looked at me a bit puzzled figuring me no doubt for a big pair. No way could he figure me for a pair of aces.

Jimmy dealt. We played five card stud with the last card up so I waited and saw that my next card was an ace of hearts. I had trips now. I had three aces and I had to have Durrico dead to rights. I barely glanced at his last card. It was a three of spades.

So there I was with three aces facing Durrico's three of spades, six of spades and king of spades. I looked at Durrico and bet. "All in."

He looked at me his large dark eyes focused on mine. He was a couple of years older than me but it was easy to see that he lived hard. His skin was rough from years of cigarette smoking and scotch on the rocks and little deep sleep. He wore a white linen white shirt more expensive than my entire wardrobe which consisted of a sports jacket and slacks with a short sleeve black shirt. Though we had been there for hours the shirt was still clean and his thick wavy black hair was perfectly coiffed despite us being out all night and into early Monday morning.

"I raise," he told me. "Ten grand. Ten grand more to see my hole cards."

I was thrilled. But I was short. "I only have five grand," I said.

He half-grinned. "You're good for it, no?"

I was quiet. I looked his cards over. He had three spades. I had three myself. There were only seven left in the deck. Did he actually have two more? This was a big time bluff and anyway, how could I lay down three aces in five card stud?

"What a bluff, man," Mikey Delarosa said.

"Nice Charlie, nice," Hilly shot in.

I glanced to the window where the guys put up a bed sheet to keep out the light. The motel room was small and I felt it getting smaller. "Ten grand more?" I asked. So that was it. If he had the flush I was down my six grand and ten more. I had nothing in the bank. Nothing. Plus I'd owe Charlie Durrico ten grand. How could he have the flush?

I moved in my chair. I reached for my scotch and downed what was left in the glass. I looked back at Durrico. He hadn't moved a muscle in his face. I eyed his gold watch, his gold pinky ring and his manicured nails. I couldn't lay down three kings. Sometimes life is like that, you can't throw away a great hand even if you are second best. I nodded. "Call."

He turned over his hole cards, the nine and ten of spades.

The stomach dropped. My head opened up. The guys cheered Durrico but he was quiet and to himself only smirking in victory. He nodded to me to turn over my hole cards. I did. He saw the aces. "Bad luck," he said.

I got up. "When do you want the money?"

"By next Sunday night is good," he said. He then took an envelope out. He poured a line of coke on the table. "Take a hit, you need it." I pulled my own straw out of my jacket pocket that hung over my chair. I did the line. I raised my head. I felt white heat blast through my sinuses into my brain cavity. I lurched back. The cocaine blew the cobwebs out of my skull but it didn't help with the sting of losing ten grand in one call.

I walked to the door, opened it and quickly left.

Once outside I was blasted with morning sunlight that felt as if it took off the top of my head. I fell against the wall and took a breath. I searched for my seventy-six green pinto, the one with the exploding gas tank, and found it in the parking lot. I got into the car, found my sunglasses and drove off.

I drove home listening to morning radio trying not to remember I owed Durrico ten grand and had one week to pay him. I fought morning traffic, people on their way to work, while I was on my way home to sleep. I opened my glove compartment amazed that I still had a twenty dollar bill I left there.

I had been teaching English in a Catholic High School in Jackson Heights but I got fired three weeks earlier. I got fired for missing more classes than I taught. At first I blamed the school for being so strict with my schedule but I knew it was all about the free cocaine that prevented me from getting to 8 a.m. classes and my spending all night back rooms in neighborhood clubs playing poker and doing lines.

I had been working on a novel about my grandfather who killed a Nazi spy on the Brooklyn docks where he was a security guard back in 1943. He was a hero and look at me.

When I got home, I took the elevator up to my sixth floor apartment and closed the windows despite it being May and already warm. I got undressed, found my ear plugs and got into bed. All I wanted was silence.

FIRST DATE
BY ERIC STROMSVOLD

"**I** need to get back to my apartment and shoot myself," Rebecca yells to her date. Billy doesn't hear her. "Do you hear me? I'm going to kill myself after I screw out your brains and throw you out like a piece of rotten meat."

Between Doc Holliday's jukebox and the table of six, who have yelping a dog with them, it's too loud for Billy's drunken ears to hear Rebecca's drunken call for help.

Rebecca had the gun ever since she first moved to Manhattan at the tender age of 20 (some 25 years ago). It was a gift from her very first New York boyfriend after getting mugged and beaten her very first year in the city. She doesn't know if the gun will even fire. She'd never fired it, and hadn't shot a gun since she left Texas, but thinks it'll be like riding a bicycle. It'll all come back to her with one squeeze of the trigger.

When Rebecca was given the gun, there were dangerous junkies and their aggressive dealers all around her building on East 11th Street and First Avenue day and night, and at the time, Rebecca was merely a terrified girl who moved from Texas after realizing she couldn't take life with her abusive father any more. She was either going to kill him or get the fuck out, so she left the farmland and never looked back. But the memories of her father and the subsequent beating haunted her nightly, and though she tried, Rebecca hadn't come to peace with her past and was in a deep depression, having suicidal thoughts fifteen drinks in on a Tuesday night with her 22-year-old date.

"I hate all this new music. It's not real punk rock. It's just sissy little crap about somebody's parents getting divorced. It's meaningless," she tells Billy, who is rubbing her thigh and leaning in for a kiss. He doesn't give a shit what she has to say. Rebecca, to him, is nothing more than another notch in his bedpost. "Kiss me," Billy slurs.

Rebecca laughs, "You're nothing but a drunk kid." But she accepts Billy's lips.

"I love the curve of your hip," Billy shouts into Rebecca's ear.

"Grab your jacket. I'm taking you home," Rebecca shouts back, before ordering two shots of blackberry schnapps that they down before heading out the door.

The East Village isn't as dangerous as it was when Rebecca first decided to call it home. Nobody has tried to rob her there since she flashed the gun in 1990 during an attempted robbery. She hasn't even carried the gun in 15 years. Rebecca looks up at the trees along the quiet, peaceful street, and laughs.

"You see this street here, Billy? When I first moved here, there was nothing but tents and cardboard boxes lining the sidewalks with people living on the street. Now people are handcuffed for sleeping on the sidewalk when they're too drunk to walk home. It's tyranny these days."

Billy wonders what the hell this chick is talking about. He doesn't want learn about the past or have a discussion on Socioeconomics. He just wants sex and doesn't want to let her diatribe kill his libido.

Billy grabs Rebecca's hand and says, "Kiss me under this streetlight."

They kiss the kind of kiss that is full of caressing, has visible tongue and makes people passing wish the pair had waited to begin until they were behind closed doors. After the kiss, Billy tries to be smooth by spinning Rebecca in a half-assed dance move that sent her tumbling out of control and this turns her stomach full of beer and blackberry schnapps to violence. She stumbles over to a parked BMW on First Avenue and projectile vomits all over its hood and the driver's side door. Billy sees his dreams of this night's lust shatter with each heave that eventually turns dry.

Billy holds back Rebecca's hair and smiles, "You're going to be okay."

Rebecca can't speak just yet but she shakes her head yes, grabs Billy's hand and pulls him along First Avenue to East 11th Street. They turn left on the corner and Rebecca begins to ramble on again just as if she hadn't just puked a night of alcohol all over some rich asshole's car.

"See that fire hydrant," she begins, pointing near the curb, "Some lady was killed there once while walking her dog. There was an electric cable exposed. She died right there, I saw her. It was terrible. Now, nobody cares. Look, there isn't even a plaque to honor her It's as if that lady didn't even exist, but I remember her here."

Billy gets Rebecca to the front door of her building which he recognizes by the staircase through the glass at the end of the hall, recalling how he'd been so excited when he first caught glimpse of Rebecca at the beginning of the night as she sauntered down the stairs wearing thigh high black boots, a short black skirt, and a black leather jacket. Now, the chance of sex with her tonight was getting slim.

Rebecca fumbles with the keys on her keychain. She has well over a dozen keys, despite only one lock on this door and two on her door upstairs. She can't find the correct key and hands Billy her keys before leaning against the brick wall.

"Can you look through them and find the one that has three jagged spikes close to where you would hold the key, and has what looks to be the head of a sperm whale at the tip? My eyes can't focus," Rebecca says, and then knocks on the door and laughs like a madwoman, "That's the key to this door."

Billy fumbles through the keys, desperately trying to find the one that looks like a sperm whale so he can get Rebecca in the lobby and then ditch her there, not giving a damn if it takes her two fucking hours to figure out the keys to the door upstairs. He finally finds the sperm whale, slides it in, turns the lock and tries to give Rebecca a short hug goodnight.

"You can't leave yet, Billy," stammers Rebecca. "Be a good date and walk me up to my door."

Reluctantly, Billy walks her up the stairs to her second floor brown steel door. Rebecca grabs Billy's head, pulling him down for a kiss. Her mouth tastes like a mix of sulfur and three-day old roadkill, but soon Billy's booze-filled brain doesn't taste a thing. He simply enjoys the make-out session that Rebecca began and pulls her caressingly close.

"You've been a good date," Rebecca praised. "Now come inside and fuck me."

Her small L-shaped studio has a bookcase full of vinyl, cassettes and CDs. Another bookcase is filled with the likes of Eliot, Hemingway, and Bukowski. She puts on her iPod and the two awkward, would be lovers, sit on the fold-out couch that also doubles as Rebecca's bed.

"I want to relax a few minutes before we turn my couch into a bed," Rebecca taunts.

They kiss some more as Rebecca's top is opened, revealing spectacular breasts. Billy cups them in his hand and starts licking. He's in heaven and becomes quite aroused and releases his grip of Rebecca's breasts so he can unbutton his jeans and pull his hard cock out. As he does this, Rebecca leans forward, crying—disappointed because she doesn't really want to have sex one last time before putting the gun to her head.

Billy doesn't notice her tears as he puts his left hand back on Rebecca's breasts, and starts jacking himself off with his right. The music drowns out Rebecca's moans and the dark room swallows up her tears as Billy pulls himself to completion, shooting sperm all over the couch that doubles as her bed.

Rebecca manages to hear Billy's moans of ecstasy over the music, turns, and looks at Billy's cock and then his eyes. "What did you just do?" Rebecca squeals with a quiver in her voice, tears caught streaming down her cheeks by the streetlight bleeding into the apartment. Billy spots Rebecca's tears and assumes that she's upset because he just came all over her couch and bed without her getting any pleasure in return.

"Nothing!" lied Billy.

"Listen, I know your junk is out, but I really don't think we should do anything."

Based on the erratic behavior that Billy witnessed from Rebecca tonight, he thinks that if she turns on the lights and sees his cum spread all over her couch that doubles as her bed, she might very well chase him down East 11th Street with a butcher's knife like a psycho. So Billy zips up his junk, grabs his jacket and bolts from the apartment just as she turns on the light.

Halfway down, Billy hears a loud bang, which causes him to assume that Rebecca is shooting at him after finding her coach/bed covered with globs of his manly essence. He bolts out of the front door and runs for his life towards Second Avenue in a zigzag fashion as he attempts to avoid getting shot. Billy doesn't look back because he doesn't want to see Rebecca chasing after him with a gun. He jumps in a cab, crouches down and looks back. Much to his surprise, he doesn't see Rebecca anywhere.

WOUND

BY KAT GEORGES

Once a week or so, in the late afternoon, Lizzie Gray found herself wandering into Our Lady of Pompeii: a nice, medium-sized church in the heart of the village at Carmine and Bleecker. Inside, a beautiful dome mural above the altar depicting Our Lady of the Rosary floating with the baby Jesus in the clouds above wretched refuse. Stained glass windows, white marble columns, dark oak pews. A musty coolness.

Lizzie was raised Catholic, and still—by habit—dipped her fingers in holy water near the entry and genuflected briefly at the back of the church. Then she inevitably crept to a dim back corner, to kneel at the feet of Saint Rocco, and pray.

O Great Saint Rocco, deliver us, we beseech you, from contagious diseases and the contagion of sin.

Saint Rocco was a defender against disease. His statue shows him with his faithful dog on his right side, while his left hand points to a festering open sore on his upper thigh. A bleeding wound. A gash. A slice nearly to the bone. A souvenir from the plague.

Saint Rocco was known to cure sick people who pray to him. Lizzie was not sick. But everyone she knew seemed to be. So many pills, pale faces, coughs, stories.

In her weekly vigil, she lights a candle, kneels on the hard worn out wood kneeler, says the prayer to Saint Rocco, stands up slowly, smashes a folded ten or twenty in the slit on top of the locked metal donation box, and heads off to work or dinner—or wherever people who are sick go these days. Which was everywhere.

Lizzie sat on a bench in Father Demo square facing north. She called it the "Hook Up Bench." She always met someone here, usually neighborhood folks, unemployed, sitting on benches to kill time when they got sick of the TV. Lizzie had no great love for anyone from the neighborhood. They were old, and made no effort to cover it up. She was not even 40—half the age of most of the local denizens. She sat on a bench reading a book, and when one of the old folks shuffled near her, she smoked a cigarette to keep them away.

She wasn't waiting for neighborhood small talk.

Lizzie sat on the bench in Father Demo square, day after day, waiting for strangers to find their place near her. Strangers her age, preferably male; more or less sane. She didn't seek them out. She thought about this often. "It's not my fault," she murmured to herself. "They choose me."

Lizzie did not smoke cigarettes if a stranger sat down. She did not want to drive them away. She wanted to draw them in, incorporate them into the circle of herself. Make herself necessary to them for a moment, a few minutes, hours, days. It was difficult at first. She had to learn to finesse her technique. To seem needy, but not clingy. To seem desirable, but incomplete. To become the focus of their attention.

Different strangers required different techniques, but the basics were the same. She had learned how to let them appear to start the conversation, by making a nonverbal comment. When they sat down, she might giggle at something in the book she appeared to be reading, then glance over at them with an inviting grin. Or maybe, on a warm day, she'd yawn, then purr. Again with the smile. Other times, she would pull a delicious apple from her purse, slice it gently, then offer the stranger a piece with a quick gesture. All simple things. In the beginning, she was often surprised at how little effort was required to start a conversation, especially if she kept her mouth shut. Magic.

This week had been slow. It was fall, perfect New York autumn weather. When the weather is nice, people like to be outside, but they don't tend to sit alone. Couples and small groups of friends milled around the square's fountain. Families crowded the benches. Her bench, the Hook-Up Bench was full for a while: she had to wait for an overly-attentive mother and two ill-mannered twins to finish their effort half-eat, half-spill some horrible-looking purple-tinted frozen yogurt and leave. The rats were going to have a real treat with the toppings that bounced to the concrete below the bench. Lizzie saw a curious rat stick its nose out of a nearby bush while the brats were still on her bench. She was about to mention this to the mother, to get them to leave quicker. But they all suddenly grew very quiet and stiff, stood as a group and marched off on cue.

The bench was hers.

She immediately lit a cigarette to deter a few locals who had been hovering about. Then, for good measure, she coughed loudly, and did her best to look ill, just to ensure privacy. It worked. Of course.

She kept her eye on the park entrance, to check for newcomers that fit her needs. What a beautiful day. Too bad. She waited for nearly an hour without spotting a single prospect.

Then she saw him. The perfect him.

He entered the park, holding a slice of pizza on a paper plate in one hand, and an awkward, medium-sized brown cardboard box in the other. In order to eat the slice, he would have to sit down. He looked hungry, and a bit worried. Every bench was full except Lizzie's bench. The Hook Up Bench.

She made herself small and the empty space on the bench looked inviting. He smiled a little, readjusted the box, and ambled toward her. As soon as he sat down, he put the box on the empty part of the bench—no doubt some leftover frozen purple yogurt still there underneath the box. He leaned forward, grasping the plate with his left hand, then picked up the slice in his right hand and ate. Happy as a giggling boy.

He finished eating, wiped his mouth and looked around the park. Slowly, slowly, his gaze drifted toward Lizzie. She was ready.

It was an old trick, but it worked. She dropped something. He picked it up. Their eyes met. He was hers.

The conversation wound like a slow, unimportant stream. The words didn't matter; only the outcome. After an hour, they stood up and left the park together. Not holding hands, not even in stride. Just two newly-introduced strangers, walking side by side.

They strolled up Bleecker, crossed Seventh Avenue, then Grove. To him they were wandering. But Lizzie knew exactly where they were headed.

Something caught her eye on 10th Street. They turned, heading west. She mentioned the Hudson, the pier; with a hint of romance mentioned sunset. The sky was already turning pale pink. Perfect timing.

They wandered past the West Village brick apartment buildings, and well-kept 19th century houses, wandered

past small cafes and galleries, wandered to the end of the
street at the Westside Highway. Crossed at the light, and as
they did she took his hand in hers. He didn't remove it. Her
hand felt like a small apple. Nice.

The pier seemed peaceful enough. There were a lot of
young people gathered on the grass, a few couples strolling
the surrounding sidewalks. Lizzie guided her new man to the
very end of the pier. Water of the mighty Hudson lapped at
concrete pillars below. Across the Hudson, Jersey City glowed
in the sunset rays. To the left, she pointed out the Statue of
Liberty, looking like a tiny mermaid from this distance.

The sun was below the horizon and the clouds in the sky
were going through their shifting pastels. New York sunsets
were softer than tropical ones, a welcoming gesture, a
promise of pleasure in the evening ahead.

In those rose-gold moments after sunset, the day seems to
be a sigh away, and the night a mystery waiting to be lived.

Staring at the horizon, they didn't notice the small group
of kids that had encircled them, until one, a tall, muscular
boy of 17, the one they called Slide, stepped up and tapped
Lizzie's shoulder.

"Cell phone. Money. Everything. Now."

Lizzie and the man twisted to stare at seven faces of all
shades and gender.

"Hey, now. . ." the man started. Lizzie shut him up with
a glance.

"I don't have a cell phone," she said.

Slide grabbed her purse roughly. "Let's see . . ." He held
up for the others. "Little lady say she got no phone. We
gonna believe her?"

"Dump it!" shouted a greasy-haired dark girl with
tattoos on both hands. "Family need money so we can do
big party tonight."

"I'm not lying," cried Lizzie. "I don't even have any money . . . well, hardly any." She tried to grab her purse back from Slide; he easily held it just out of her reach.

"Dump it!" shouted a skinny red-haired boy with a scar on his cheek. "The more they say they ain't got nothing, the more shit they do got!"

"That right," said a wideset, low-voiced girl with a shaved head. She slapped Lizzie's face hard. Lizzie screamed sharply. "Ain't that right, bitch?" She slapped her again, and Lizzie fell to the ground, whimpering.

Slide stared hard at the man Lizzie was with. "This your girl? Why you ain't doing nothing about that whack-out she getting?"

The man mumbled something about never hitting a woman. The low-voiced girl cackled and slapped him, twice, and twice as hard. He growled with pain, bent over, grasping his face.

Slide bent over, too, shouting, "Where your phone? Where your money?"

Still bent over, the man pulled his iPhone from his jacket pocket, and a handful of neatly folded bills from his jeans. Slide grabbed them both. The other kids started dancing and singing.

"Oh, yeah . . . uh-huh, uh-huh . . . we all right now! Oh, yeah . . . un-huh, uh-huh . . . we party all night now!"

Slide opened Lizzie purse and turned it upside down, shook it. Nothing fell out. Nothing was inside. He grabbed Lizzie's hand and helped her stand up, then gently handed her purse back.

"You truth-teller. You all right. Better get out of here now, lady."

Lizzie grabbed her purse and ran back down the pier as fast as she could, without looking back even once. She

ran and ran, until her air ran out, then she walked
fast down familiar streets, her legs on automatic, refusing
to think at all.

She arrived, and pulled open the big door. Dipped her
hand in the water. Felt the coolness of the dim space under
the vaulted ceilings. Turned to right, to the back corner,
knelt, prayed.

*O Great Saint Rocco, deliver us, we beseech you, from contagious
diseases and the contagion of sin.*

She was still praying when she felt a light tap on
her shoulder.

"Hey . . ." someone hissed. It was Slide.

"Not here," Lizzie whispered. "Wait till we're outside."

"Not this time," the voice hissed. "Right now. We got of
take care of something right now. But first—here's your cut."

Slide handed her a stack of neatly folded bills. She
counted quickly, three fifties and a c-note. Two-hundred
fifty dollars. Not bad. "How much did he have—cash?"

"Thousand," Slide said. "Must've just cashed a check,
something. And the phone was the latest sty-lee. All told we
net a thousand cash, so 250's your cut."

Lizzie knew he was lying—they must have scored at
least fifteen. She saw the size of the wad back in Father
Demo square. But two-fifty was fair. In fact she was relieved
to know the kids—her project, her adopted family—would
be off the street tonight, out of harm's way, instead of troll-
ing johns in cars on Weehawken, risking it all for a few dollars. Risking contagious diseases and the contagion of skin.

"Glad it worked out, okay, Slide," she said, rising. "Do
the right thing for the family tonight."

Slide gently grabbed her touched her shoulder. "Can't
leave yet, Liz—we got to talk about a complication.
Here. Now."

She looked at his face, and for the first time in the two years she'd known Slide, he looked a bit worried. No, seriously worried.

"What?"

"That man you were with . . ."

"Yeah?"

"Something happened and umm. . . we . . . umm . . . we had to put him in the river."

"You threw him in the Hudson?"

"We had too! He was . . . he was . . . something happened—and he, like, croaked."

"Who did it?"

"What you saying? Nobody did nothing! He did it all on his own."

"I don't believe you, Slide!"

"What the fuck? You think I did it? Just cause I'm the big guy? You coming down on me? If anyone did it, you did, and you know it. Wouldn't be nothing wrong without what you did."

"I didn't do anything. I was just taking a walk with him, and was attacked by a vicious wolfpack of violent youth."

"So that's what you think we are? We just kids! And we the only ones who saw what happened down there."

"Oh, come on—I only come down there to help you out! Keep you out of the shelter—off Weehawken! I'm keeping you alive, goddamnit!"

"Why you want to keep a vicious wolf pack alive? Huh?" Slide was growing strangely quiet in the dim, dank air of the church. "You want to pet us? You want to tame us? You want to take credit for saving us? You trying to feel less guilty?"

"I'm sorry, Slide. I didn't mean any disrespect. You know I love you like my own children."

"You say that, you must be the she-wolf. You ain't so innocent. Don't ever forget that. And when you be reading the papers tomorrow, seeing the body they find, seeing that man again, you better not be thinking about telling any story to anyone, unless that story starts with "I" and ends with "did it."

Slide grew even quieter now, and brought his mouth next to Lizzie's ear.

"And one more thing. Just to make sure that we don't start telling one stories about what You did, I think we better change a few of the ways we do business. I'm talking, business between you and me. I got to make some major payouts to keep our little monsters on the right track."

"Okay, okay, okay," Lizzie said. "I know, I understand."

The church door opened and a group of tourists entered, and stared around.

Lizzie whispered, "We can't do anything in here. Too quiet. Meet me outside, in the park, on the Hook-Up bench. I'll be there in five minutes. We'll figure something out. I'll make it worth your while."

"Five minutes," Slide echoed, and left.

Lizzie kneeled again in front of the statue of Saint Rocco.

O Great Saint Rocco, deliver us, we beseech you, from contagious diseases and the contagion of sin.

So many sick people. Everyone except her. She'd help Slide out. She'd help everyone. She knew another pier, further downtown. The moon was so beautiful from there. Hardly anyone knew about it. Just her, and another small group of street kids that she helped out once in a while. Her other adopted family. She loved everyone of them madly, as if they were her own.

ABOUT THE AUTHORS

RESA ALBOHER is one of the founding editors of *St. Petersburg Review* in a variety of publications including *Maintenant 5* (Three Rooms Press), *Scapegoat Review*, *DMQ Review*, *Faggot Dinosaur*, and *Black Heart Magazine*. She currently lives in Moscow, Russia, but her heart equally belongs to that Gotham City between two rivers, NYC.

L. SHAPLEY BASSEN was a finalist for 2011 Flannery O'Connor Award and is Fiction Editor for prickofthespindle.com, a reader for electricliterature.com, and a book reviewer for brooklyner.org, the rumpus.net, and bigwonderful press.com. She won the 2009 APP Drama Prize & a Mary Roberts Rinehart Fellowship.

LAWRENCE BLOCK first visited New York in December of 1948. He and his father stayed three nights at the Commodore Hotel, rode a double-decker bus and the Third Avenue El, saw *Where's Charlie?* on Broadway, and attended the live broadcast of the *Ed Sullivan Show*. He never got over it, and a few years later he began living in—and writing about—his favorite place on earth.

RAE BRYANT is the author of the short story collection, *The Indefinite State of Imaginary Morals* (Patasola Press, 2011). Her stories have appeared or are soon forthcoming in *StoryQuarterly*, *McSweeney's Internet Tendency*, *BLIP Magazine*, *Gargoyle Magazine*, and *Redivider*, and have been nominated for the Pen/Hemingway, Pen Emerging Writers, and Pushcart awards.

SION DAYSON is a New York-born, North Carolina-bred writer living in Paris, France. Her work has appeared in *Utne Reader*, *Hunger Mountain*, *Numero Cinq* and the anthologies *Strangers in Paris* (Tightrope Books) and *Seek It: Writers and Artists Do Sleep* (Red Claw Press), among other venues. Sion holds an MFA in Writing from Vermont College and blogs about the quirkier side of the City of Light at paris (im)perfect. Links to more of her work can be found at siondayson.com.

KOFI FORSON is a writer based in NYC. He has written and directed theatrical plays at The Riant Theater, and the co-author of *Dismember the Night,* a collaboration with artist Dianne Bowen of photographs and poetry which premiered at Tribes Gallery. Currently he writes for *Whitehot Magazine of Contemporary Art.*

JEB GLEASON-ALLURED was born in Wheaton, Illinois and lives in Brooklyn. He recently completed his first novel and can be found at jebgleasonallured.com.

JANET HAMILL is the author of five volumes of poetry and short fiction. Her most recent collection *Body of Water* (Bowery Books) was nominated for the Poetry Society of American's William Carlos Williams Prize. Her poem "K-E-R-O-U-A-C," originally published in the anthology *Bowery Women,* was nominated for a Pushcart prize. She has recorded two CDs in collaboration with the band Lost Ceilings. She is an artist advisor at the Seligmann Center for the Arts in Sugar Loaf, NY and is studying for her MFA in Poetry from New England College.

RON KOLM is a member of the Unbearables, and an editor of several of their anthologies; most recently *The Unbearables big Book of Sex!* He is a senior editor at *Evergreen Review* and contributing editor of *Sensitive Skin* magazine. He is the author of The Plastic Factory and, with Jim Feast, the novel Neo Phobe. Kolm's papers were purchased by the New York University library, where they've been catalogued in the Fales Collection as part of the Downtown Writers Group.

MARIA KRANIDIS teaches at Suffolk County Community College. Her work has appeared in *Cabaret, State of the Art, Rio, Cassandra, Confrontation, Poetry Magazine, Best Poem* and *Apollo's Lyre.*

PETER MARRA has had over 100 poems and several short stories published either in print or online. A Dadaist and Surrealist, his earliest recollection of the writing process is when, as a 1st grader, he constructed a children's book that included illustrations. The only memory he has of this project is a page that contained an illustration of an airplane, caught in a storm, drawn in crayon. The caption read: "The people are on a plane. It is going to crash. They are very scared."

PUMA PERL is a performance artist, poet and writer. She is the author of the full-length poetry collection, *knuckle tattoos,* as well as two chapbooks, *Belinda and Her Friends* and *Ruby True.* She was the co-creator, co-producer, and main curator of DDAY Productions. Her newest venture is Puma Perl's Pandemonium, where poetry meets rock n roll.

THOMAS PRYOR's work was published in *The New York Times, Mr. Beller's Neighborhood, A Prairie Home Companion,* and other periodicals. His blog: "Yorkville: Stoops to Nuts," is listed in *The New York Times Blog Roll.* In 2010, Thomas appeared on public televison's acclaimed series, "Baseball: A New York Love Story and featured on public radio's "This American Life." His first book of photographs, "River to River—New York Scenes From a Bicycle," was released by YBK Publishers in 2012.

MICHAEL SCHWARTZ is a writer, actor, director, solo performer, humorist, educator, singer, and drawer. His poetry is published in the new anthology book, *Slices of the Apple: Voices from the New York Performance Poetry Circuit.* Among the awards he's won for his writing was the Interpreting Brooklyn grant from the Brooklyn Historical Society, for his short stories, poems, monologues, and songs set in Coney Island. Schwartz is director of the Adult Ensemble of PLAI Theatre, a new non-profit arts organization for people with disabilities.

JACKIE SHEELER, poet and songwriter, has lived in NYC all her life.

ERIC STROMSVOLD is a native New Yorker. "First Date" is his first published short story.

RICHARD VETERE wrote *The Third Miracle* (Simon & Schuster) and co-wrote the screenplay adaptation starring Ed Harris, produced by Francis Ford Coppola and directed by Agneiszka Holland released by Sony Pictures. His plays include *Caravaggio* and *One Shot, One Kill.* His new novel *The Writers Afterlife* is forthcoming from Three Rooms Press (2014).

EDITORS

PETER CARLAFTES is an NYC playwright, poet, and performer. He is the author of 12 plays, including a noir treatment of Knut Hamsun's *Hunger*, and his own celebrity rehab center spoof, *Spin-Dry*. Carlaftes is the author of *A Year on Facebook* (humor), *Drunkyard Dog* and *I Fold With the Hand I Was Deslt* (poetry), and *Triumph for Rent* (3 plays). He is co-director and managing editor of Three Rooms Press.

KAT GEORGES is an NYC poet, playwright, performer and designer. She is the author 12 plays, including *SCUM: The Valery Solanas Story* and *Art Was Here*, a creative look at Dada instigator Arthur Cravan. She is also author of the poetry collection *Our Lady of the Hunger*. In New York since 2003, she has directed numerous Off-Broadway plays, curated poetry readings, and performed widely. She is co-director and art director of Three Rooms Press.

books on three rooms press

POETRY

Hala Alyan
Atrium

Peter Carlaftes
DrunkYard Dog
I Fold with the Hand I Was Dealt

Joie Cook
When Night Salutes the Dawn

Thomas Fucaloro
Inheriting Craziness is Like
  a Soft Halo of Light

Patrizia Gattaceca
Isula d'Anima / Soul Island

Kat Georges
Our Lady of the Hunger
Punk Rock Journal

Robert Gibbons
Close to the Tree

Karen Hildebrand
One Foot Out the Door
Take a Shot at Love

Matthew Hupert
Ism is a Retrovirus

David Lawton
Sharp Blue Stream

Jane LeCroy
Signature Play

Dominique Lowell
Sit Yr Ass Down or You Ain't gettin
  no Burger King

Jane Ormerod
Recreational Vehicles on Fire
Welcome to the Museum of Cattle

Jackie Sheeler
to[o] long

Angelo Verga
Praise for What Remains

George Wallace
Poppin' Johnny
EOS: Abductor of Men

PHOTOGRAPHY-MEMOIR

Mike Watt
On & Off Bass

FICTION

Michael T. Fournier
Hidden Wheel

Richard Vetere
The Writers Afterlife

DADA

Maintenant: Journal of
Contemporary Dada Art & Literature
(Annual poetry/art journal, since 2003)

SHORT STORIES

Have a NYC: New York Short Stories
Annual Short Fiction Anthology

HUMOR

Peter Carlaftes
A Year on Facebook

PLAYS

Madeline Artenberg &
Karen Hildebrand
The Old In-and-Out

Peter Carlaftes
Triumph For Rent (3 Plays)
Teatrophy (3 More Plays)

Larry Myers
Mary Anderson's Encore
Twitter Theater

TRANSLATIONS

Patrizia Gattaceca
Isula d'Anima / Soul Island
(poems in Corsican with
English translations)

George Wallace
EOS: Abductor of Men (American poems
with Greek translations)

three rooms press | new york, ny
current catalog: www.threeroomspress.com